Lasting Summer

kailin gow

A New Adult/Contemporary Adult Loving
Summer Novel

Kailin Gow

Lasting Summer

Published by THEEDGEBOOKS.COM

THEEDGEBOOKS.COM is an imprint of

Sparklesoup Inc.

For information, please contact:

THEEDGEBOOKS.COM c/o Sparklesoup Inc.

11700 W. Charleston Blvd., 170-95

Las Vegas, NV 89135

www.theEdgeBooks.com

First Edition.

Printed in the United States of America.

ISBN: 978-1597481113

Thank you!

Thank you readers for loving this series and helping me mold it through the polls you answered on theEDGEbooks.com. Also, a Big Thank You to the Betas who gave me feedback about Summer's decision before Lasting Summer was published. It is always hard to make these decisions especially when both sides feel so passionate about their favorites, but in the end, hopefully many of you will be happy.

Prologue

Nat's Letter to Summer

My Perfect Summer,

I hope you will and can forgive me.

I never meant to hurt you, but sometimes we do things because we thought it was the best or only way out.

I don't know where to begin. But if you are holding this letter in your hands, then I know you already have a sense of what this is about.

Again, I am writing you a letter not because I am old-fashioned, but because this time, it was necessary. It was the only way I can get word out to you that I am okay. That I am alive.

I can't have you suffering over grief for me, thinking I was dead. I am in the sense I could not be with you in more ways than one.

I will always love you, Summer. You are the world to me, but circumstances have changed. I don't know if I will ever be the same Nat as you loved. If I could return to be the Nat that you could be with. Sometimes in the line of duty, you are forced to do things that you would not be proud of. There were a few things I had to do in order to get the job done. But I did it, and because I did, my father will be on his way back home.

Will I come home soon? It depends. I don't know when or if, so that's why I'm writing you this letter.

Please go on living life to the fullest as you always have. Go on and be as happy as you can be, and don't put your life on hold for me to be happy. I know how you feel about Drew, and I know how Drew feels about you. With me no longer there for you, please turn to Drew for support. He knows why I'm doing this, and he knows how to comfort you best, as well as how to protect you.

Life is too short to wait for love. I am so grateful for the chance we had together. I take those memories with me everywhere I go, but it is now time for me to let you go, and for you to let me go. I love you with all my heart so I am letting you go to fulfill your destiny, as I am doing so now.

Love Your Nat in Shining Armor for Always

Summer

I've read Nat's letter again hoping to find some clues as to his whereabouts.

I should be happy he's alive, which I am, but he's put me through hell and back again when I thought he'd died. I mean I was in such despair, Drew even found me sitting in a bath tub with a razor blade nearby. I've never sunk so low to consider taking my own life out of despair.

Me. Summer Jones, the one everyone turns to for warmth and happiness. How can I be the Summer who have provided the Donovans the sunshine and warmth they depended on me for when I was now filled with darkness and pain?

Nat had deceived me. Drew had deceived me, and now I was truly all alone.

Nat Nat Nat! Why did you disappear like that? What are you hiding?

I know Nat. He wouldn't pull something like this on me unless he absolutely had to…which led me to believe he may have believed there was no other way. But why? He knew I loved him with all of me since we were toddlers. I handed him my heart on a silver platter everyday hoping he would notice the love I harbored for him, believing he was my entire world. How could he lead me to believe he was dead? How could he leave me and take away my choice as to who I should love?

And Drew, the fact that he knew Nat was alive, yet saw me cry and grieve for him, saw me sink to the point I nearly lost my mind, so I can fall harder for him, choose him over Nat… I was so furious with him, I told him I didn't want to see him ever again.

I meant it too.

It's been two weeks since I last saw him in person, since I last spoke to him. Despite him calling me every day, texting me, and even showing up to the Pad; I've shut him out. The old Summer would have answered his texts and phone calls the first time and forgiven him, while apologizing to him for something he did. The new and current Summer? I needed time to step back, step away from his intoxicating sexy body and presence to think, to clear my mind.

I've resisted the temptation to answer him, to feel any contact with him through his words, his voice, or sight.

Until now…

His text to me couldn't have come at a more opportune time.

DREW: Summer? I'm through begging you for forgiveness. If you won't believe me, maybe you will believe Nat. I know you've been inquiring about him. If Nat is who you want, I will find him for you.

I took a deep breath before hitting reply.

ME: This had better not be some kind of joke, Drew.

DREW: It isn't. I never meant to hurt you.

ME: You did.

DREW: I'm sorry. It seems all I wanted to do is protect you, but it has the opposite effect instead. I hurt you. Can I see you at the Pad tonight?

ME: Can't.

DREW: Why not?

ME: Too many memories of us. Too many memories of Nat being here. When I see you again, I want to see you with fresh eyes.

DREW: I'm sorry I let you down, Summer. I will do whatever it takes to make you trust me again.

ME: Show me Nat is alive. That's how.

I sighed. Although it was just his texts, I imagined hearing his voice saying all of this to me. I missed talking to him. I missed the close bond we've had since we were kids. I missed feeling his hot skin next to mine as my lover, and I especially loved hearing his voice. Loved how he said my name. Whenever he did, it sounded like he cherished the name as much as he cherished me. He'd always had a way of saying my name that made me get butterflies in my stomach.

DREW: Come to my new place then. Meet me tonight?

I hesitated again, but knew I had to see him, to finally get this out into the open and talk. If he knew where Nat was, then I need to see Drew.

ME: Okay, just to talk.

DREW: I promise. We'll talk. I'll pick you up at the Pad at 5.

ME: 5 is fine.

DREW: Wear your summer dress…it's my favorite outfit, Summer.

ME: We're just talking.

DREW: We'll be talking, but that dress is so spectacular on you, and I love how it brings out the sunshine in you.

I had to smile. That was Drew. Can't blame him for trying.

ME: I'll surprise you then. Maybe I will or maybe I won't. See you at 5.

With that, I turned off my phone and hopped into the shower. I'd nearly forgotten how easy-going we were together and how he was my best friend with whom I could talk to about everything before we became more than friends. Shutting him out after what he did to me was hard. Not only was I losing the man I loved, but I also lost one of my dearest best friends.

Now I don't know what we are anymore, but after what he did, it would take some time before I could even trust him again. It would take some time before I could trust anyone again.

Chapter 1

<u>Drew</u>

I didn't want to be part of the "plan" that Nat and Dad cooked up to help Nat disappear. It wasn't even my idea, and I felt bad about the whole thing. I didn't want to go with it at all, especially about having to withhold the truth about Nat's whereabouts to Summer, who was going through so much grief over Nat. It killed me to see how she took to the news that Nat was dead. Not because I was jealous of how she loved Nat, but because I could see the light, the warmth of her, her personality and soul dying. Although it was bliss for me to have her to myself, at the same time, I felt and shared her pain.

If it was up to me, I would've told her the truth

when she first found out Nat was missing. That's because I know Summer. She wouldn't want anything less than that, despite how much it would hurt. Nat disappearing for her sake took the choice from under her...she never got a fair chance on which Donovan Brother she wanted to be with since Nat took that choice away from her by stepping out of the picture and wanting her to be with me.

But I couldn't tell her. It would jeopardize the safety of Nat, my father, and even Summer's mother.

As much as everyone thinks I would be elated about having Summer be with me, I wasn't. That wasn't closure to her, that only fueled her insatiable inquisitive mind to find out what happened. And coming from me, she wouldn't believe me. She needed to hear it straight from Nat. That is how she is...she won't accept anything less than that.

Nat? Thank God he was alive, but now comes the complicated part...I can see Summer's pretty mind working. If Nat is alive, why isn't he coming to see her? Why hasn't he contacted her? It is worse knowing he is intentionally and deliberately shutting her out of his life. Now she needs to know why. She won't move on until she finds out why.

So…I have to find my bastard of a brother. Yes, he was a bastard even in the literal sense. Now I'm furious with him. Furious for putting me in this situation with Summer. Furious for now making himself incomparable to Summer. No man can live up to Summer's memories of Nat. No matter how much I try, no matter how much love I give her, how much of my skills at lovemaking, how much I try to be more like Nat; it isn't working. Because I'm not him.

And now I realize, no matter how much I tried to be Nat for her, I will never be Nat to her.

So, the best I can hope, if there is any chance for me, is to be Drew. The real Drew. I've been trying to be everything to everyone for so long, I don't even know who the real Drew is anymore. I guess I'll find out soon because from now on, with Summer, I'm going to be me so she will love me for me. And she will love me. I'm sure of that.

Because the real Drew Donovan is a no-holds barred, take charge, take no prisoners kind of guy. The real Drew Donovan is a beast. He will take what he wants when he wants it…including Summer. It's the real me when I take charge on the football field, it's me when I take charge in the bedroom with women I've had, who are much more experienced than Summer. I was holding back with Summer, but not anymore. She wants to know the truth? She wants the older brother just because he seems more in charge and more like a man in control, wait until she sees the real me. Given the chance at being the big brother, given the chance at really running Donovan Dynamics my way, I will unleash that part of me I've kept hidden. If Nat or anyone challenges me on being the alpha, I will not step aside this time. If it is true that Nat is Aunt Sookie's son, then I am the rightful heir and son to the Donovans. Not Nat. It had never been Nat, but me.

I looked around my new suite, which reflected more of my tastes since I was made President of Donovan

Dynamics. It wasn't the apartment of a college student. It was actually a penthouse in one of the buildings we've had near Malibu used mainly to house enormous data files. The whole setup with me here was for security reasons, because making me President of Donovan Dynamics since getting Dad back, put me at a higher risk for any attempts by the crime ring we helped dismantled. The building was near USC where I could work as a satellite headquarter for Donovan Dynamics, but also live on the top floor as a penthouse suite. Full security throughout the entire building and a place where Nat can carry out his work for dad, while maintaining his new identity as a student at USC.

Yeah, Nat was still in the picture, which made me both uneasy and at ease. Uneasy because he could take everything away from me, including Summer if he made himself known, and at ease because he could help me keep Summer safe, which I know he will if he can. That's why I think he accepted his cover as a student at USC…so he could stay close to Summer, watch out for her. That's why, despite how hard he worked to build up Donovan

Dynamics, he was willing to give that all up, give up the billions that could come with that inheritance, so he could be there for her.

In a way, I'm kind of jealous of his new identity. He didn't have to fit into anyone's expectations anymore…no more football hero, no more big brother to Rachel and I, no more caring son to Mom, and Dad's secret confidante about his ex-mistress. It's like the burden of being Nat has lifted, and he can be what he wants to be.

I haven't seen him yet since his new identity, but I will soon. For Summer's sake, I'm bringing Nat back from the grave so to speak…

Chapter 2

<u>Summer</u>

I decided to wear that white almost sheer summer dress Drew loved seeing me wear. While I was furious with him for what he's done, a part of me cared deeply about what he thought of me, that he still wanted me as much as I had to admit, craved him too.

I dressed in my sheer summer dress with the tie around halter top with green and blue embellished gemstones lining the chest and neck area. It showed off my shoulders and arms, which were toned and tanned due to hours of playing collegiate volleyball, and slipped into pearl and silver linen white wedges. I finished my look with chandelier earrings with jade and sapphire stones that brought out the green, blue and gold specks in my eyes. Then I brushed out my long thick chestnut hair, arranging it in waves which framed my face. The look was polished, sophisticated, fun, classy and sexy. All that time when I was with Astor and his entourage of hairstylists, personal stylists, publicists, and manager did rub off on me, as they taught me how to look and dress my best, especially as Astor's girlfriend.

This look would have Drew eating out of my hands. He is going to so regret not telling me about Nat when I get through with him tonight and teach him to never withhold information from me and never try to deceive me like that again.

I put on some mascara, lip gloss, and a bit of blush before grabbing my silver clutch purse and headed out of my room to the front door where I could see through the window panel near the door that a car had pulled up in the driveway.

Before Drew could get out of the car and come to the front door, I opened it and strode confidently to the passenger side door of the shiny black Audi and tried to look in. The windows were tinted so I couldn't see anyone inside, but the door popped opened with a click without anyone having to get out to open it.

I opened it further and looked inside at the driver.

His face was masked in the dark of the car, and he was wearing a black suit and black shirt without a tie. He was facing forward without looking at me, with one arm casually on the steering wheel.

Really? He hasn't seen me in two weeks, been texting me, calling me constantly, and tried to see me at the Pad a few times...so this is how he greets me? With indifference, with no show of love...almost with a huge amount of arrogance. Who did he think he was?

"Drew?" I asked.

He turned towards me then, his face coming out of the shadows and fixed me with his brilliant blue eyes. The intensity of his gaze paralyzed me for a second, as he stared into my eyes, almost angrily.

What was he angry about? I was the one he betrayed.

I touched my hair, pulling one strand behind my ear as I leaned into the car. It was Drew, only more dapper, more self-assured in a grown-up manly way that was incredibly sexy. He didn't smile. He didn't gush. He looked me over from head to toe without any expressions of approval or disdain and said, "Good to see you, Summer. Now get in."

Wow. I expected something a little warmer from Drew, but in a way, it sent a shiver of desire through me that cut through the anger I was feeling towards him. I got into the passenger seat, and before I can buckle myself in, Drew leaned over, his head of wavy jet black hair brushed my nose, and I could smell a musky vanilla scent that instantly made me clench. His fingers brushed against my breasts slightly as he pulled the seatbelt strap around me, and fastened it securely. His hands brushed against my thighs as he tested it to see if it was tight, and then he looked up, raising his face so close to mine, we were an inch away from being lips to lips.

"There," he whispered, his hot breath caressing my lips, as his eyes followed the curves of my lips up to look into my eyes. "You are nice and tight now, Summer."

You bet I am.

"Gotta make sure you are snug and secure because we're going for a ride in my new car. Got it this afternoon, and I want to see how fast it can go," Drew said before jerking the car out of my driveway and immediately accelerating to a speed that was much too fast for my neighborhood.

I found my voice again after we made it to the highway, and he was steady. "Drew? Where are we going?"

Drew glanced over at me and said, "You wanted to find Nat, didn't you?"

I nodded. I did.

"Well, so do I," he said. He gritted his teeth, and I can see his strong jaws working. He was angry at Nat, just like I was angry at Drew. We drove on for a few more minutes, and he didn't take his eyes off the road to look at me nor say anything else.

I didn't expect this about Drew at all. He wasn't at all like the Drew I thought he would be. Could it be he no longer wanted me as I wanted him? There was no denying how my body reacted to his smell, to his touch, and even to the mere sight of him. I was already reliving my hot memories of his tongue and hands on me, all over me, bringing me to ecstasy…of the times we couldn't keep our hands off each other, of his deep kisses that always left me breathless.

I watched his expert hands guide the steering wheel and felt a warm blush cover my face as I remember his hands lathering me with soap and washing me in the bathtub, of his fingers plunging into me, hitting my sensitive spot, and making me writhe in unbridle intense pleasure before climaxing. I swallowed, feeling my entire body warm up in the memory of Drew touching me, kissing me, and making love to me. I leaned back in my seat, involuntarily arching my back and pushing my breasts forward while closing my eyes. Those memories were so intense, I almost feel as though it was happening now.

I must've moaned when I opened my eyes in surprise, remembering where I was. I glanced over at Drew and saw the dark hungry look in his eyes as he looked over at the area where my dress hem ended halfway on my thighs. His eyes traveled up to my chest and cleavage then to my mouth. "Had a good nap?" The corners of his mouth turned up into a small smile.

"I didn't even know I fell asleep," I said.

"From the sound of it, you were in deep sleep and dreaming about something that was making you moan and touch yourself," Drew said, his eyebrows cocking slightly. "I can only imagine what that could be or who you might be thinking of..."

I blushed, looking into his eyes and turning away quickly. "I haven't slept very well lately. It could have been anything. Maybe even a nightmare."

Drew laughed. "I doubt that."

For some reason, his laughed riled me up a bit. Why was Drew being so distant to me? It was like that time he said he only wanted to be friends. Is that what this is?

I leaned up and turned towards him. "You are so sure of yourself, Drew," I said. "So sure you know me that well that you think you're the one I just dreamt about."

"I never said that," Drew said. "Now you're being presumptuous. What makes you think I would even be with you in your dreams. Or for real? Cocky, aren't we?"

"Maybe," I said. "Maybe I was dreaming about going down on you, running my tongue up and down on um Little Drew, while squeezing you tightly with my hands, taking you deep into my throat until you explode. Or maybe I was riding you reverse cowgirl-style while your hands play with my breasts and we keep thrusting until we both climax?"

I glanced down at the front of his pants, and noticed how a large unmistakable bulge was now making it tighter, Drew had to readjust his pants. I almost giggle knowing what I was doing to Drew just by talking dirty to him. Bet he didn't expect that from sweet Summer. Touche, Drew for pulling on this indifference to me act. Two can play this game.

Drew sucked in a breath and said, "That's quite a picture, Summer. Maybe you can make a career out of being a phone actress?"

"Maybe you can make a career out of being a gigolo," I shot back.

"Why?" Drew asked. "Thinking about sampling my services?"

"I've already sampled your services, and well..." I shot him a heated look. "I could survive without it."

Drew's eyes widen in complete surprise.

There. I got him now. Truth of the matter, he was an incredible and passionate lover...I couldn't get enough of him, and everything about him makes me heat up inside, including this banter going back and forth.

"Really?" Drew asked. His eyes burned into mine. He licked his lips. "As I recall, Summer, you can't seem to have enough of me. You always have multiple orgasms when we have sex."

"Really?" I asked, cocking my eyebrows.

"You can't possibly be faking all that, all those throaty moans and passionate cries…" Drew looked shocked, almost pale at the possibility that it can be true.

"Women do it all the time," I said, feeling some triumph in chipping away his armor of indifference towards me.

"Not with me," Drew said. "Definitely not between us."

"Are you sure?" I asked.

"I can tell if you're faking it or not," Drew said. "I didn't just get known as having the Drew Effect on women for no reason. None of them ever complained."

Now I was stumped. His mentioning other women sent a wave of jealousy through me, which I couldn't help. Drew did have that effect on women everywhere. He was constantly given slips of paper with phone numbers or email addresses from women. For a guy that handsome, with his tanned muscular physique, nearly jet black hair and deep blue eyes; there was never a shortage of women he could have. Women practically threw themselves at him in the most embarrassing way. In terms of experience, he was very sexually experienced, and no doubt he could tell when and if a woman was faking an orgasm.

I was quiet for a moment, remembering how I hated how he was such a player, how he could be so casual about sex. This was before he and I became more than friends. Then things became so complicated with me dating Astor, then Nat, and then finally Drew until I threw him out of the Pad and broke up with him two weeks ago.

"Summer," Drew had stopped the car, parked it into an underground garage in a large building and turned off the engine. He turned to face me and used his hand to cup my cheeks before pulling me towards him. "I shouldn't have brought up the other women," he said softly, looking into my eyes. "I'm sorry."

"I…"

"That look on your face just now, Summer," he said searching my face with his intense blue eyes, "You still cared." His eyes darted to my lips as I nervously licked them.

"What if I do?" I said softly, almost breathlessly.

"It means I'm not sorry for this." He pulled me in for a kiss, crushing his full lips against mine, while his tongue delved in to take mine. I hungrily kissed him back, relishing the feel of him against me, the smell of him engulfing me, his arms around me as it had always been – strong and protective and now possessive. Drew groaned as my hand accidentally brushed against the front of his pants. "Summer, what are you doing to me? These last few weeks without you…" he kissed me again, harder and more passionately.

I kissed him back, relishing in the feel of him against me, his skin against mine. He was so warm, so passionate, I could feel the heat of his body chase away the hollowness and pain in me. I sighed. Since he, Nat, and their sister Rachel came back to Aunt Sookie's Malibu Pad for the summer a couple of summers ago, and the Donovan boys had noticed me; my body had craved Drew's touch. He really was sex on legs.

He had unbuckled my seat belt and reached his hand under my dress and between my thighs, his skilled fingers reaching for his prized possession where he rubbed and tantalized me to the point I was writhing against him. "Drew," I panted. "We have to stop."

Drew tensed for a moment and looked up from where his mouth was kissing the top of my breasts, while his fingers worked me from below. "Stop?" he asked, his eyes looking incredulous. "Right before I..." he pulled one of my breasts out from my dress where it was bare and took it into his mouth to lick and devour.

I was moaning my head off.

"Should I stop now?" Drew took a second away from licking my breasts to ask.

"No, no, don't stop," I panted.

Drew took one long lick of my nipple before he pulled away. "You're right, we should." He ran a shaky hand through his hair and took a deep breath. "I'm sorry. I promised we'll just talk so…I'm sorry I got carried away."

He opened the door of the driver's seat to get out of the car and came around to my door, opened it and reached for my hand to pull me out.

He held my hand as he closed the door and led me to an elevator, where he stuck in a key and pushed a button that was marked "P".

"Where are we going?" I asked, looking up at Drew.

"You'll see," Drew said, standing behind me so closely that I can still feel his desire for me pressed against my back.

I was still a little frustrated with him for getting me so riled up just to stop abruptly. It was cruel. Didn't Drew know how every time I'm near him, it was as though all my nerve endings become alive? My senses, my skin grows alert in anticipation of his touch. With Drew standing so close behind me, clearly as aroused as I was, I pressed my butt against the front of his crotch and pushed backwards to pin him against the wall while I rubbed my butt in circles around his hard-on.

Drew groaned, "Oh that feels good, Summer."

I rubbed faster moving my hips in circles and then up and down.

"God Summer, keep this up, and…"

The elevator bell rang and I launched forward, leaving Drew bent over with a raging hard-on.

I looked around where we had stopped, thinking we would have an audience when the elevator door opened.

No one. The elevator doors opened into a small hallway that led to two large grey non-descript doors.

Drew came up from behind me, took my hand, and led me through the doors and into a luxurious modern-style straight out of Architecture Digest penthouse suite.

"Where are we?" I asked again.

Drew led me to the middle of the living room furnished with expensive soft leather Italian sofas, plush angora area rugs and glass tables. "This," Drew said, gesturing all around him, "is my new place."

"Really?" I asked.

"Really," Drew said. "I know you were expecting something different for me, but all this comes with the territory of having been promoted by Dad to President of Donovan Dynamics."

I swallowed. That position was Nat's. Did that truly confirm that Nat had given up everything about his old life, including a stake in the company he helped built?

I looked around. The place looked so sophisticated, elegant, and upscale. Not at all like the Drew I knew.

More like Nat.

"Where's Nat?" I asked. "You're lying Drew, this isn't your place. It's Nat's. So he's been hiding out here? Now, where is he?"

Chapter 3

Summary

Drew smiled slowly and calmly said, "Summer, this is my place, and this…all this is also who I am."

He walked over to the double door steel Sub-Zero refrigerator, opened it and grabbed a chilled bottle of water out, placing it on the large marble-top kitchen island. He bent down and pulled out a pot, filled it with water, turned up the stove, and placed the pot on top of the fire.

"Bet you're hungry," Drew said. "I'm making dinner. You can make yourself comfortable while I cook. He took off his jacket, placing it on the back of one of the chrome and leather barstools at the island, then rolled up his sleeves. I watched him confidently navigate through the kitchen, taking out pots and pans, vegetables, spices, and other ingredients.

In his black shirt that hugged his broad shoulders, muscular chest, tight rippled abs, and strong arms; he was incredibly sexy, taking charge of the kitchen. He looked up at me and smiled. It was his beautiful Drew smile, filled with happiness and charm. He was happy being here, cooking dinner, having me here with him. Despite how angry I was with what he'd done, I couldn't help smiling back at him. I loved seeing him happy.

He poured the vegetables he chopped into the pan he fired up, stirred it a little, then covered it with a lid, before washing his hands, drying them and then taking out two wine glasses which he filled with the water from the expensive-looking water bottle he took out. He walked over to me and handed me one before sinking into the sofa seat next to me. He took a sip of the water and placed it on the glass top table in front of us. He watched me as I took a sip, and he took away the wine glass to place it on the table next to his. Then he turned to me, and cupped my chin, turning my head to face him. "Believe it or not, Summer, all this is mine. Since Nat left, and I had to step up to be the one in charge of Donovan Dynamics, in charge of my family and looking out for you, it made me grow up. I was into football, into modeling, and caring only about sex like a lot of guys my age, but when I found out more about what my father and Nat had built up with Donovan Dynamics, about losing people you love and about love, it made me think about a lot of things. Including what I really wanted, who I wanted to be, and what I want my future to be. I'm not that irresponsible playboy you thought I was…the Drew who disappointed you, who don't deserve you. I wanted to be a better man for you. I want all this, Summer. I want you, too." His lips crashed onto mine, kissing me with a force that made me leaned back into the sofa while he pressed into me. My head began swirling as all I could think about is Drew kissing me like he couldn't get enough of me. All I could feel was his hands touching, caressing my legs up my thighs and now in between my legs.

"Oh Drew," I sighed, kissing him back, matching his fervor kiss by kiss.

"Summer," Drew said, between kisses. "You're the only girl I've allowed to come here. You're the only person I've brought here. This place, Summer, this entire building, is mine, and you will be all mine, too. You are the only girl I've ever loved."

I felt his hand fist around my panties and with one tug, he had ripped it off…just a strip of cream lace and silk lying in a heap on the rug next to us. His two fingers plunged into me, hitting the most sensitive part of my entire body and causing me to gasp.

Drew smiled. "I'm going to give you a Drewgasm right now, before I return back to check on the pasta primavera I'm making."

I was about to say something but Drew took out his two fingers from where he had been rubbing me to the point I wanted him to fill more of me. He stuck his fingers into my mouth where I can taste myself. "You taste incredible," Drew said, taking his fingers back out of my mouth and sticking it into his, where he licked them one by one, closing his eyes and savoring each lick. "I could lick you forever. I miss the taste of you, Summer, because it's you."

"Hungry? I am, and I'm going to start with dessert first." He pushed me all the way down, tilted my hips up, pushed a cushioned pillow under my hips, and kissed me on my folds. As soon as his hot wet tongue licked me, I nearly jumped out of my skin. It was electric hot, sending tendrils of pleasure all over my body. I moaned, grabbing Drew's thick wavy black hair, pulling him closer to me. He increased the pressure of his tongue and circled the area around my clit, making me wanting more.

"Drew...I want..."

"What do you want?" he growled.

"You to not stop," I breathed.

"There's no stopping me, Summer." His mouth enclosed on my entire vaginal area into an intimate kiss, while his tongue continued stroking my clit.

I grabbed the pillow behind my head and arched my back and felt my entire body trembled.

He moved his mouth to kiss my clit and suck hard on it, taking my breath away. Without stopping his fingers from touching me, he grabbed my hips, squeezing my buttocks while he pulled me closer to his face and hungrily sucked and licked me until I was crying his name. "Drew, oh Drew," I moaned. "I missed you…"

"Summer," he groaned, wrapping my legs around his shoulders and lifting my bottom up while he continued hungrily devouring me. "You're so wet, so turned on…" he stopped massaging my hips and stuck two fingers in me sideways, turning them gently inside of me until he was palming me and stroking my sensitive g-spot, while his thumb stroke me up and down.

The sensations exploded around me, and my body was whacked with strong tremors, jerking up and down, while I ran my fingers through Drew's hair.

He groaned, as he showed his arousal, but continued his relentless onslaught on me.

I felt another tremor go through me, making me bite down on my lips. "Drew, this is. Too. Much."

I cried out in pleasure and my eyes opened in wild ecstasy as he placed two more fingers in me, while continuing to lick and devour me. He turned his hand and slowly pumped me, pressing down in an area that made me feel full, and then his tongue rimmed my folds, licking up and down. His forehead rested on my clit and began rubbing it, brushing it with his hair.

It was the most arousing, incredible sensation that made my nipples harden, my eyes rolled back, and my stomach clenched. "Oh my God, Drew!" I cried. "I..." I felt another clenching and then my stomach and entire body tighten, before an explosive climax thundered through me. It whacked me for a few more seconds, making me writhe so hard, I nearly knocked Drew off of me.

When I subsided, my face was flushed, and I was panting, but felt so relaxed.

I opened my eyes, and Drew was facing me, his hard-on so hard in his pants as he rubbed against me slightly. He took my face into his hands and kissed me hard, then softly, his beautiful blue eyes looking deep into mine. "I love you so much, Summer," he said softly. "Whatever I did to lose you, I'll make right. Just please give me a chance..." he kissed me again, and I felt something wet on my cheeks.

Drew's eyes were still intensely on mine, but there were tears that had escaped onto his cheeks.

He softly pushed a strand of hair from my face when he pulled back his face to stare at me, to look at my lips, my cheeks, and then my eyes as though he was memorizing me. "When you said you never wanted to see me again, Summer, it nearly broke me. I thought I lost you; I thought I lost everything." He took a deep breath. "It was a feeling I'd never want to have again, Summer."

He kissed me again, resting his cheeks on mine, and stroking my hair. "I'm sorry I didn't tell you about Nat, Summer. I'm sorry I was too much of a chicken, too much of a good son to my dad, to hold such a secret from you. It killed me to see you go through everything you did, thinking Nat was dead, when I knew he wasn't. I couldn't let you know. I was told if I did, it would put everyone I love in danger. Especially you. I couldn't risk you being in danger too from those guys who were after Nat. I'd rather you end up hating me than being on their hit list, especially after what Nat and your mother did."

I pulled up. "My mother?"

"She was the real reason why Nat went on the mission…to get her out. My father promised Aunt Sookie he would do everything he could to look after your mother and you before Aunt Sookie passed away. She was on a dangerous mission, and was taken hostage."

I sat straight up now and adjusted my dress as Drew got up. "Tell me more."

"I will, but I have to check on dinner." He pulled me up on my feet and led me to the dining table off the side of the kitchen island. He pulled a chair for me, seated me, and ran to turn off the stove, and lift the lid of the pan he was simmering.

The rich scent of tomatoes, herbs and spices, filled the room, and I heard my stomach growl.

"Looks just about right," Drew said, taking dishes out of the cabinet, draining some pasta, and preparing the dish.

He scooped out the steamy sauce and added it to the pasta, and washed his hands before grating a block of cheese on top and then chopping up some cilantro to add a pinch to the dishes.

With a smile of satisfaction, he brought two plates out to the table, placing one in front of me and another in the seat at the front of the table next to me, where he sat down.

He placed a napkin over his lap before he unfolded another to place on mine, brushing his hands over my still sensitive crotch area, sending a thrill through my body. He pulled back, stopped, and smiled his typical and lovable Drew smile that I missed so much.

"As I promised, Summer, here's dinner, and some Drewgasms before dinner."

His smile widen, as I felt a blush cross my cheeks. "You certainly delivered on those promises, Drew," I said thinking about how incredible his Drewgasms made me feel just moments ago.

"And I'll deliver on more promises, Summer," Drew said, taking my hand. "Including you begging me to make love to you again, including me making you mine and only mine." He looked confidently into my eyes and said, "Now eat up. We have a lot of things we need to do tonight."

Chapter 4

I had nearly forgotten how good of a cook Drew was, but with one taste of a spoonful of pasta with sauce that he fed me, my mouth was filled with an explosion of flavors.

"Oh, this is so good," I said. "How come you've never made this dish when you were staying at the Pad with me?"

"Because Summer," Drew fed me another spoonful, and then licked the rest of the spoon. "I make dishes from the places that inspire me. At Aunt Sookie's Pad, I made dishes that reminded me of summer days, of beaches, of the sea."

"And this place?" I opened my arms gesturing all around me. "What does this place say to you?"

"It's another stage in my life, Summer," Drew said. "It's the part of me who enjoyed traveling to new places. It's the part of me who love beautiful and luxurious things that comes with being the son of a billionaire. It's also me, who is stepping up to become the son my father wanted me to be, to lead Donovan Dynamics one day."

Drew looked away for a second before facing me again. "I'm not trying to be Nat for you, Summer. I know you think this is more like Nat's style than it is me, but I'm letting you know right now, this is just another side of me that you haven't seen much of before."

I blinked and stared at him, not yet sure what he wanted me to say. Do I want the old Drew back? I've always loved him, but deep down inside, I did wished he would grow up a bit, show more depth than just the gorgeous hunk of a football hero that he portrayed to everyone, including his own family.

I leaned back into my chair and took a good look at Drew, noticing how his black shirt and slacks gave him a sexy sophistication and a sense of danger that was irresistible. It brought out the brilliant blue of his eyes, as well, which stared back at me with a vulnerability that showed that he cared a whole lot about what I thought.

"If this is you being you and not Nat nor what your father expects, then I love it," I said.

Drew let out the breath he was holding. "Thank God," he said, getting out of his chair to go down on his knees to wrap his arms around me in the kind of hug he always gave me. "I can't go back to being like I was before...always the little brother hiding and waiting in the wings. Just Rachel's twin brother. As much as I love Nat, Summer, I love finally being the one my parents turn to...the one being taken seriously for once."

"I always took you seriously," I said.

"I know," Drew kissed me on my lips. "That's why you're so different than everyone else. That's why every word you say to me, every gesture you gave me, growing up and even now, meant so much to me. You are my everything, Summer. When Aunt Sookie's stalker Sloane came after you that one time and I found you just in time, I wanted to kill him for terrorizing you and almost raping you. If you hadn't stopped me, I probably would have. Now these guys who took your mother hostage and then my father...they're ten times worst."

He closed his eyes.

"Summer, the reason I didn't tell you about Nat is because not only would it put Nat, my dad, your mother in danger over there, but they would have come looking for you too. Sloane was just one small part of their criminal ring, and the work your mother and Donovan Dynamics were doing, helped shut down that part. But it's bigger than that. It's a larger problem than anyone knows."

The look in Drew's eyes was dead serious as he let all that sink into me. I could only register part of what he was saying, as the enormity of what Drew was saying hit me. "Oh God," I said. "Nat had to disappear, fake his death so that he could live."

Drew nodded.

"And you, Rachel, your mother, and the Team at Donovan Dynamics all had to act like it's the truth in order for it to work," I went on.

"These criminals are the masters of deception, Summer," Drew said. "They can smell the setup a hundred miles away if it isn't authentic."

"So me being closest to Nat, being his girl…they were watching me, weren't they?" I asked

"Like a hawk. You know how Sloane was able to get private photos of you, was able to take photos of you everywhere, even in your shower at the Pad?" Drew looked angry for a moment. "Even posed as a fellow college student in our class?" Drew's eyes flashed. "That's how close they can get to you."

I shuddered, remembering how Sloane had stalked me, how he had vandalized Aunt Sookie's Acting Academy's theater…everything. It was just too close for comfort.

"So me being with you…me and you making love for the first time when I was at my lowest and you found me in the bathtub…that was all part of the plan? Did Nat want all that too?"

"Nat made me promise him that I will do whatever it takes to protect you."

"Did he want me to be with you? To have us make passionate love with each other that entire time I was in grief over him?"

"It had to look real, Summer, that you were grieving him, that you had moved on, to me," Drew said. "But no, it wasn't what Nat wanted. It couldn't possibly be what he would want. But it happened, and what happened between us while we were both grieving him, was real. Every time I kiss you…every time I make love to you, is real."

"But how did you get from barely knowing anything and being mildly involved in Donovan Dynamics to now being able to run Donovan Dynamics? You seem to know your way around pretty well."

"I wasn't completely left out of learning about Donovan Dynamics growing up," Drew said. "I worked there on and off throughout the years, especially when Dad needed all of us kids to help out in the beginning."

"The superficial Drew who only cared about one-night stands and football? Was that an act, too?"

Drew grinned, "No, not at all. That's just who I was then. You caught me then and saw through that façade. But it sure made me look non-threatening to them so I guess it wasn't all that bad."

"No, it wasn't," I smiled. "I fell in love with that Drew, but this one…it's growing on me…"

"Glad this one is growing on you," Drew said. "I wouldn't want to disappoint. But listen, Summer, there is a real good reason why I brought you here tonight instead of anywhere else."

I stared into Drew's blue eyes, demanding him to tell me the truth.

"Whatever we say in here, whatever we do, it's surveillance-free. We've been swept for bugs, viruses, whatever can be used by the crime ring. This suite here is on top of Donovan Dynamic's new secret satellite office. It also provides a way for me, Rachel, and now Nat to be down here as college students with you in Malibu."

I couldn't believe my ears. Did I hear right?

"You just said Nat was here too?" I asked.

Drew blew out some air. "I shouldn't have said that."

"Is he here?" I asked again.

Drew looked down and said, "Shit. I blew that one."

"Drew?" I asked, taking my hands to hold his face so he's looking me in the eyes. "I've been through so much the last few months worrying and grieving over Nat...at least tell me something...is he here in Malibu...so so close to me?"

Drew's eyes held mine as he said those words that he knew could cause him to lose me forever. "Yes."

As though right on cue, the doorbell rang, causing both Drew and I to turn our heads so fast to look at the door feeling both dread and excitement.

Chapter 5

I wanted to run to the door and yank it open, but Drew put a hand on my shoulder, silently telling me he would check on the door. His jaws clenched tightly as his anger with Nat took over, and he walked towards the door in strong strides. From the way his hands balled into fists, I was expecting a fight.

I got up and walked calmly over to stand behind Drew as he opened the door. If there was a fight brewing between the two brothers, I was going to be there to stop it, knowing and fearing someday, they may end up killing each other if I was not around.

Keeping me safe from Sloane was one of the reasons the brothers bonded again after Nat and I got together and Drew went missing. Also, there was a bond we all shared, having been raised by Aunt Sookie, who was my biological aunt, but who took the Donovan siblings under her wings. When she died, the bond was still there, but it had been tested many times.

Drew, always Drew, had been there for me.

Always there…picking me off the floor.

Oh how I've been so blinded by my own hurt to see that Drew was only keeping Nat's secret in order to protect me.

I gently touched Drew's shoulder and leaned in to kiss his cheeks, surprising him enough to stop from opening the door, ready to pounce on Nat. "Drew," I said, looking up into his eyes, "I understand. It wasn't your fault, and I'm sorry I blamed you all this time. I'm sorry I shut you out of my life for the last two weeks after I received Nat's letter. I was consumed with grief over Nat, and then to find out it was all something you, Nat, and your father came up with to deceive me, I couldn't take it any longer So you see, Drew, I didn't mean to have all that pain explode on you when you came to see me. I shouldn't have blamed you. You were just as much as a bystander as I was.

Nat and your father always had a way to make you go along with their plans. I realize now how it isn't your fault…it couldn't be. You were just there to pick up the pieces Nat left of me. He should be the one I never want to see again. Not you. You've always been there for me. I just never saw through my blindness to your love and kindness."

Drew's hand fell off the doorknob, and he turned around, wrapped his arms around my waist, and pulled me to him. "Summer," he whispered, his eyes filled with agony but love. "You don't know how long I've waited to hear you say that to me." He crushed his lips on mine in a kiss that made my toes curl and my head spin. How long we had been kissing, I didn't know, but when we finally pull apart, Drew cupped my cheeks and said, "I love you Summer Jones. You are the most precious person to me. I don't ever want to be torn away from you again!"

I took his hand and pressed it against my cheeks, "I can't stand not having you a part of my life, Drew. It tore me apart being away from you these past two weeks as it did when I lost Nat. I became someone filled with darkness, bitterness, and anger…someone I don't want to be."

"Summer…" Drew kissed my forehead, then took my hands, kissing the tips, before he poured kisses all over my face. "Summer," he said, pressing harder against me, turning me around so my back was to the wall next to the door. He raised my arms above my head with his right hand, and lowered his head to kiss my neck, my shoulders, and the top of my cleavage before returning his sweet lips to devour my mouth. "I want you so badly it hurts. I've been holding back because you asked me to respect your wish to just talk, but…"

I was flushed from being against Drew's delicious body, from his hot kisses, and electrifying hands. "I want you too…"

Drew groaned and lifted me to wrap my legs around his waist. His hands cupped my bare butt, my panties already torn and beyond repair lying on the rug near the sofa. "You are so aroused, my dear Summer," he grinned. He lifted me higher until my thighs were sitting on his strong broad shoulder, and my lower half that was craving him so much, faced his sweet full lips. "Hold onto the wall, Summer," he said, taking a step back so my folds opened up to him invitingly. "There," he said. "So beautiful and sweet. I wanted to savor my dessert, but with you, there is no way I could take my sweet time with you. You are the one I crave, Summer. Your taste alone satisfies me." His mouth covered my entire lips with a deep kiss that made me almost lose my grip on the wall.

"Drew!" I cried. "Oh Drew..." his hot tongue circled my lips, before he plunged into me.

I closed my eyes, relishing his onslaught on me before my body was overfilled with pleasure, it exploded with tremors all over. Drew slid me down to hold me while my body continued shaking. "How do you feel?" he asked afterwards.

I leaned into him as he stroked my back. "Hmm?"

"I guess that means you enjoyed it," Drew said looking at me with adoring eyes.

"How could I not?" I asked. "I'm putty in your hands. When it comes to you, Drew, my body becomes your puppet to do with it as you please."

Drew laughed. "I like that!"

I shook my head, "Oh no," I glanced at the door. "I was just trying to keep you from killing Nat, but we got caught up in it...I can't believe I keep losing my head when it comes to you, Drew..."

I grabbed the doorknob to open the door, twisted it and swung it open to reveal a hallway that was empty.

Drew stepped up next to me to look up and down the hallway.

I ran out to the elevator. "Maybe we can catch him downstairs. Oh no, I can't believe I missed him."

I punched the elevator door, and had it go down to the first floor of the building. Why? I had no clue where Nat went or even if he lived here at the building, too. But I went down to the ground floor, got out of the elevator and looked around. Like the entire building, except for the top floor, which was Drew's penthouse suite, the entire place was empty of people.

"Nat?" I called out? "Nat?"

I walked around the lobby area, hoping to see any signs of someone. It was night, and only a few lights were on in the building. I walked down the hall towards one office that looked like there was a light on inside.

I quietly turned the knob of the door to open it when a hand touched me on my shoulders, causing me to jump.

"There you are," Drew said. "You ran so fast for the elevator, I didn't get a chance to catch you. What are you doing down here?"

I looked down. What was I doing down here? Snooping? "I wanted to catch Nat. If he left the building wouldn't he had to exit from the first floor?"

"Summer," Drew said, cupping my chin so I was looking at him. "I'm afraid that wasn't Nat at the door. I forgot to tell you I have security, just one man sometimes who check up on the building. Make sure things are fine. I think that was just Jim checking up on me."

"Oh," I said. "I thought you said you would find Nat…that he was here."

I couldn't hide my disappointment.

"He was supposed to, but somehow he didn't," Drew looked as disappointed as I felt. "But you know what, Summer…maybe there was a reason, a good reason, because now you understand why I did what I did to you."

I couldn't help feeling I let Nat down now, though, although Drew and I had cleared things out. Did Nat actually show or was it really the security guy checking up on Drew. If it was Nat waiting at the other side of the door while Drew and I were talking, kissing, and together; he would've heard everything.

Chapter 6

Drew

All he had to do was show up. That was all I had asked of Nat so Summer could have her closure…so she could move on and finally let herself go with me.

But the guy didn't even have the balls or decency to face us.

Summer was heartbroken about Nat's deception, and I was left to pick her up, even left with feeling the brunt of her despair. There was no one else she could turn to, yet the two closest people to her who held her fragile heart in their hands twisted it and deceived her. It was a testimony to her generous heart, that she was able to find love for me once again.

But then again, I broke her trust. I promised her Nat, and he didn't show. I don't know what she'd think…that I made up all this about Nat showing just to get Summer to see me, to open herself back up to me just to have it go crashing down?

I drove Summer back to her place soon after I found her on the first floor, which was actually the second floor. At the new building, the first floor was the basement, where we had top secret information in servers running in a large wing of the floor. Summer somehow found the door leading down the hallway to that wing, which had multiple levels of security.

It was a place Summer should not be visiting. I didn't want her face photographed on the security cameras leading to that area, in case there were any concerns later on. I didn't want her knowing about the place in case she gets targeted for her knowledge. It was better for her to know nothing. If she ever gets hurt or worse because of her knowledge and association with me, Nat or Donovan Dynamics, I could never forgive myself.

Why did she think about Nat right after I made love to her? Wasn't I enough to satisfy her? Why did she run after Nat with such abandon, left me behind while she pursued him?

Nat, Nat, Nat! He was the bane of my existence. Not only did he take the place of the eldest son in the family, but he took whatever chance I had with Summer, by being her first.

I called up the line that hid Nat and my true number and waited for Nat to pick up.

After a five rings when the voicemail would pick up, I heard a click.

"You asshole!" Nat's voice shouted into the receiver. "What kind of a game are you playing… inviting me to your Den, just so you can flaunt what you have with Summer?"

"So you did show up?" I asked.

"I had better things to do," Nat said, "but for the sake of Summer's sanity, I did…only to hear her tell you she never wanted to see me again! Only to hear you and

Summer…I can't even talk about it. It's bad enough I had to leave Summer, but to hear her having sex with you right when I was expecting to see the love of my life again, it's low, man. Really low."

"So you took off…again, breaking Summer's heart all over again. Just as always, Nat. You see, you can't face her. You chickened out. I admit what happened right behind the door between Summer and me would hurt you, but you had no idea how much hell you put Summer and I through. She dumped me and said she never wanted to see me again. She meant it too. All because I, being the good little brother, kept your secret. You think I wanted to see the girl I've been in love with since I can remember, crying her heart out and almost killing herself over a liar like you? And not being able to tell her the truth? She hates me now. That little scene you heard will probably be our last. She gave me the chance to prove to her I was telling the truth about you, but because of your no-show, it's back to ground zero. She thought I lied about getting you to the Den to see her, when you didn't show up. Now I don't know if she'll ever trust anyone again. You see, Nat, she trusted you and me to be there for her, to be her rock, but all we've done was play with her emotions…play with the desires we both have for her. It isn't fair what we've put her through. She's been there for us, and all we've done was hurt her. I tried to make it up to her, but I don't even think she wants anything to do with me. As much as I'd hate to see you succeed with Summer, she needs to see you."

"She won't recognize me now that I'm undercover, but I'll find a way to let her know, I'm around," Nat said steadily. "Technically, I'm not even supposed to make contact with her or see her. I can't let my cover get blown."

"You shouldn't have sent her that letter then," I said. "You either disappear completely or don't. It's as simple as that. Why do you always have to complicate things, especially when it comes to Summer?"

"Wow," Nat laughed. "Is this Drew I'm talking to?"

"What?"

"Never thought you'd have any deep thoughts beyond which girl you're going to hook up with…"

"Nat, man, you better take that back," I said, a little angry. "That was before Summer. I'm not like that anymore. I have responsibilities now…stepping into your shoes at Donovan Dynamics, taking care of Mom, making sure Rachel isn't in over her head with whatever new thing she's into…right now it's Astor or Ashton Fairway."

"Hmm, that pretty boy actor who wanted Summer," Nat nearly spat. I know him, he didn't trust Summer with him before and now he wouldn't trust Rachel trying to get with him, too. "Keep an eye on Rachel with him. I know he's helped out with Aunt Sookie's Academy, but I still think he's not over Summer. If he hooks up with Rachel, he'll break her heart."

"Still the Big Brother," I said.

"Just because I'm technically 'dead' doesn't mean I don't worry," Nat said. "And just because I have another identity doesn't mean I'm not helping Dad and Donovan Dynamics out. Listen, when I went over to the Den earlier,

I wanted to see Summer for real, and you, but I also had to go into the Vault to update some info. Nearly got decapitated just going in. You have some serious security there, Drew. Make sure you keep Summer out. I know she's too curious to stay put but you have to. If she's going to go over to your place more often, then secure the place, even against Summer. I don't want her to get hurt even more so Summer-proof the place."

"Easy for you to bark orders from far away," I said.

"Exactly," I said. "Now you know what it's like to be in my shoes."

"I'm not following in your shoes," I said. "I'm stepping up to be who I am…"

"Good," Nat said. "It's about time. Now if you'll excuse me, I have work to do."

He hung up before I could get a retort in. The tension between us was thicker than ever. Strained when it used to be so easy between us.

Even if he went back to being Nat as before, would we ever be close again?

Chapter 7

Nat

I never should have sent Summer my last letter. I should have just let her believe I was dead.

Like the rest of the world, like those dangerous criminals I help send to prison.

Like those corrupt officials and executives at unethical corporations who hired the cybercriminals to do their dirty work so they could be ahead of their competition, so they have information that could take down their rivals.

Aunt Sookie's Acting Academy was one of their targets, and so was Summer after she inherited the Academy. You'd think they wouldn't care about a small acting school like Aunt Sookie's, but they did. It was an act of revenge, because of Summer's mom.

She busted them first, then I came in, helping her through Donovan Dynamics as part of the government contract.

What I found out would blow anyone's mind.

What I found out would turn anyone and everyone into a paranoid basket case.

I intend to keep this knowledge hidden as much as I could. No one knows any of it, except me.

And Summer. She doesn't know it yet, but she will. If anything happens to me now, she would be notified to retrieve that letter I sent her. The clues are in there. Let's hope that day when she would have to read that letter again never happens. But if it does, hopefully by then, Summer would understand everything I did, everything I said was for her.

*****

I had to go see her. Although I was hurt and filled with jealousy when I heard her sweet voice talking to Drew behind their suite's door; my entire being felt more alive than these last few weeks, just being able to hear Summer's voice.

I did feel dead inside, cut off from my family, my role at Donovan Dynamics, and from the one woman I've always loved. So, it wasn't hard for me to get out of my dorm room, get into my Prius and drive up to the Pad.

It was close to midnight, but I had to see her.

I was so familiar with the drive to the Pad, as well as the Pad itself, I could navigate in the dark towards her house. I parked across the street from the Pad when I got there, as to not draw any attention. If someone was watching her, they wouldn't notice anything unusual.

Dressed all in black, I blended into the night that surrounded the Pad, took out my own key to the Pad and walked in.

Immediately the memories of me kissing Summer, holding her tightly against my chest as I said, "good-bye" to her hit me. How much I dreaded leaving her that day to go on a mission I may not survive. If I hadn't gone, I would be sleeping next to Summer at this moment, caressing her, holding her and making love to her.

Oh how I missed her...her warm soft skin, her happy smile, how her beautiful gold-specked green eyes light up every time she saw me.

I made my way from the front door to the living room where Summer, Drew, and I grew up watching television together, playing video games, and hanging out.

Pass the cozy, but large granite-top kitchen where we've played and cooked meals for each other.

To Summer's bedroom where I once undressed her and made sweet love to her.

I held my breath as I laid eyes on the sleeping form underneath the blankets. Even in deep sleep, she was the most beautiful girl I've ever seen. Her beauty still takes my breath away.

I walked up to the bed and watched her sleep for a moment, enjoying the tranquility it brought me. "Summer," I whispered. "Summer, I'm here. Nat."

At the sound of my name, Summer sighed in her sleep. "Oh Nat," she said, her eyes closed. "Kiss me," she said, grabbing my hand and pulling me down towards her on the bed. I fell next to her as she leaned into me, "I'm so cold," she shivered. "Nat, cover me up with your body so I can feel the warmth."

My arms fell around Summer, pulling her in close to me. The feel of her in my arms, the heavenly fresh floral scent of her hair, struck me with the need to have her, to feel her entire body next to mine.

"Kiss me, Nat," Summer said, searching my face with her hands as she leaned in to kiss me. Our mouth crashed into each other with a hunger I thought I'd buried the day I left this Pad, the day I left Summer.

Now I'm back, and my girl Summer was back in my arms. I closed my eyes overwhelmed with emotions and lust for Summer.

She had full delectable lips I wanted to bite and suck on. "Oh Summer," I groaned. "I should never have left you. How could I leave these lips?"

"Go ahead," Summer said, "Make love to me. I've always wanted you, now I need you. Please."

"Oh Summer," I kissed her again and ran my tongue down her neck to the top of her tank top. I had to smile. When she was with me, she went to sleep naked with me, but now…she was back to being the Summer I knew before she got mixed up with me or Drew. Maybe that was a good thing. It showed she wasn't with someone at the moment. It comforted me, knowing she still cared for me.

"I love you, Nat," Summer said, her eyes closed as in deep sleep. "I used to dream about being your girlfriend.

I used to believe we were destined to be together. We are, and since you died, I can't go on unless I join you…I can't imagine my life without you."

I stopped kissing her and looked at her face closely. She was breathing, she was paler than the last time I've seen her, and right by the side of the bed on the side table was a bottle…a bottle of pills.

"Oh no, Summer," I cried, grabbing the bottle and shaking it. No more pills were left. "Why?"

Frantically I began pumping her chest, which made her cough. A few pills came out of her mouth. I looked at them and saw multicolored ones of animal shapes. I picked up one and relief poured all over me. They were gummy bears.

I laughed. It was so like Summer. My sweet adorable Summer. And I bent down to check her breathing. It was steady, and her eyes were still closed. I looked at the bottle next to her and saw it was a bottle of sleeping pills. She didn't seem to have taken too much, but whatever amount she did, it knocked her out, and she was in deep sleep, only acting out her dreams.

Again, I was relieved she didn't take those pills to kill herself.

I didn't want to take advantage of her in this state so I pulled her tank top down to cover her up and just laid next to her, holding her gently, letting her know I was there for her.

I soon fell asleep, but woke up at the crack of dawn to slip out of the Pad. I couldn't leave at first, but stood just watching her sleep. I thought about how scared I was when I thought she took too many pills.

And what she said while dreaming. That she would follow me wherever I went...it terrified me.

"Summer, I know you're still sleeping, but please forget about Nat. Please move on with your life, find someone new...like Drew. Especially Drew. Please give him another chance..."

I kissed her on the forehead and left.

Despite everything, she was still and will always be my perfect lasting Summer.

Chapter 8

<u>Summer</u>

So he was also in my Sociology class. What did I expect?

My eyes swept over to where Drew had entered the stadium-tiered classroom at USC where we were both entering our second year. He was dressed in a dark navy suit that hugged his muscles and a black silk shirt opened at the neck. His hair was combed yet mussed up as though he'd just had sex. I didn't notice it as much last night because I was so focused on the tension between us, but in this light, his hair had grown longer to his shoulders in a way that gave him a rakish pirate look. The slight blue of his navy suit brought out his blue eyes, and made him look like he'd just came out of a Jane Austen novel.

He was gorgeous.

Looking at him made me want to grab his head to run my fingers through his hair.

I wasn't the only one noticing how gorgeous of a male specimen Drew was.

A flock of pretty girls, as usual, jumped out of their seats to surround him, touching him, flirting with him, grabbing him.

"You'd think they thought he was Astor Fairway," I muttered under my breath, getting ready to get up to go 'rescue' Drew from the girls.

"Can a Peacock get any more vain?" A handsome young man about nineteen or twenty sat down next to me. Although he was dressed in baggy skater boy clothes, the laid-back casual California attire preferred by many of the guys in college, with a cap scrunched over his bleached platinum hair; I could tell he was very good-looking.

Trying not to turn my head to openly check him out, I glanced at him from the corner of my eye. He was tall, had long legs and broad shoulders. Sitting next to him, I felt his strong presence, although he himself seemed laid-back without a single care in the world.

I laughed. "He seemed to be enjoying himself," I said watching Drew charm his way with the girls. I was about to go help him out but just watched him. He was used to his Drew Effect on women of all ages, and he knew how to work it. One girl was handing him a pen, while another was massaging his shoulders.

"Yup, he does," the gorgeous man next to me said. "I'm surprised not all the women in class are over there joining his harem. The guy's one charmer, isn't he?"

"Yes, if you're into that kind of thing. I don't do harems. A guy who seemed so into himself like that just doesn't do it for me."

I watched Drew get kissed on the cheeks from a girl who I recognized as the President of a sorority. Drew had belonged to a fraternity last year and been a star quarterback on the football team on a scholarship and on early admission. Of course he was prime meat for the prettiest and most popular girls on campus.

I clenched my hands into a fist as that kiss on the cheeks turned into a kiss on the lips, and Drew seemed to have kissed her back. "Uh, would he stop this?" I muttered. "I can't believe him, after all he'd said to me last night, seemed him being into me was a lie too."

I wanted to get out and storm out of the room, but the gorgeous man next to me placed his hand gently on my elbow. "He's not worth it," he said. "Don't let a man keep you from living your life. You're here to learn, aren't you? Then don't leave just because that guy missed out on an opportunity to show you he is worthy of you."

Wow, he seemed deep. I glanced over at the guy next to me to see his face, but he was half hidden to me, as he looked straight ahead. All I could see was his strong chin covered in a day's growth of stubble, his aristocratic nose and long eyelashes from his side profile. Without his cap, he'd probably be even more gorgeous than Drew, but in a rock star kind of way. "I can't watch him like that," I said.

"Then don't," he said. "Ignore him. He's an idiot for putting on this kind of show in front of you, if he thinks it'll get your attention. How do you feel?"

"Disappointed," I said. "I thought he grew up. I thought he turned over a new leaf, that he can act more responsible, more of a man whom I can lean on and trust, that he could be more like…" I stopped. What was I about to say? That I wanted Drew to be more like Nat? All this time, that was what I loved about Drew?

"What?" the guy asked, suddenly turning to face me.

"Oh never mind," I said, blushing. "I shouldn't be telling you all this. We've just met, and now you must think I'm some kind of emotional mess."

"Never," the guy laughed. "If you're an emotional mess, you sure hide it well."

"Thank you," I said. "I try. I figure it's the start of a whole new school year, I can try to start fresh, get more involved in school than I did last year."

"That sounds promising," the guy said. "Always good to start fresh if you could."

"I'm Summer," I smiled, offering my hand to him.

He turned towards me, looked me in my eyes with his aquamarine eyes, mesmerizing me for a second. The shape of his eyes, those long lashes that any girl would envy, the intensity of his direct gaze...they sent an electrifying thrill through me, yet gave me some comfort. He smiled and took my hand, engulfing it wholly. "Nice to meet you, Summer," he said. "I'm Cooper. Cooper Sorrento."

Even his name sounded like a rock star's. "So, Cooper," I said, "Why are you taking this class?"

"I was curious about it," he said, "Plus I'm interested in the way our society is and where it's heading. Especially with all the technical advances we have these days. You?"

"I was told this is the class I needed to fulfill my undergraduate requirements. Sorry, not so deep as your reason for being here."

Cooper laughed. "Well, you're here, might as well enjoy it."

"Yes," I laughed.

Cooper brought up his hand to face me, and I high-fived him, making me giggle outloud. He was exactly the kind of guy I needed right now. A breath of fresh air, a different kind of guy from Drew, Nat, and Astor. A guy who seemed to just take life one moment at a time…which reminded me of someone I used to know. Myself.

A guy who I could just be friends with. I smiled at Cooper and said, "Thanks for making me stay. I think I'm going to enjoy this class."

"Of course," he said. "Now pay attention. I think class is about to start." He pointed to the front of the room where a man in his fifties with glasses and a beard went to the podium.

"Good afternoon," he said, "I'm Professor Knapp. In case you think this is a class on sexual relationship and dating..." he coughed looking straight at Drew and his harem, which had the decency to stop fawning over Drew to sit straight ahead, "you're in the wrong class. That class is being offered next semester and being taught by yours truly."

My mouth dropped open and I looked over at Cooper, grabbing his wrist. "No way!"

Cooper laughed. "Just can't judge a book by its cover, can you?"

"Yes, um, being a Sociologist," Professor Knapp continued, "covers some of that, and you would be surprise to find we as humans, our society, and civilization are defined by our social mores towards sexuality, gender roles, and relationships. Please sign up for that class next semester if any of that appeals to you."

The harem in front of the classroom giggled, while Drew raised his hand.

"Yes, Mr..."

"Donovan," Drew said. "Will you touch on society's rules on dating, courtship, and proper etiquette, even with today's rules?"

"Very thoughtful question, Mr. Donovan," Professor Knapp said, "especially coming from a guy who, let me guess, patterns himself after Casanova?"

The class laughed.

"I just want to know," Drew spoke up, "the expectations placed on young people like us on what is proper and what isn't. You see, Professor Knapp, as an aspiring Casanova, I want to know everything there is about how to please a woman. I want to know what makes them tick, what makes them fall madly and wildly in love with you."

The harem gave a collective sigh while I took an involuntary short breath. No doubt he was referring to me. I felt a flush sweep over my face and tried to sink deeper into my seat.

Professor Knapp chuckled. "That's a pretty honest reason why you'd be interested in taking the class. I'm afraid the class wouldn't be about sexual techniques but more about society's take on sexuality and how that shapes our personal choices. As far as getting a woman to fall wildly and madly in love with you, I would say, from personal experience, it depends on the woman. As far as what to do exactly, you'd have to ask my wife what I did right."

The room laughed, and I had to admit, I already liked Professor Knapp and was interested in everything he had to say.

"Now if there aren't any more questions regarding my other class, please take out that sheet of paper my assistant passed out, marked 'syllabus'."

I listened to everything Professor Knapp was saying, finding this class more and more fascinating than I had originally thought. My focus was on him, but I saw Drew turn around after he was through with his question, and he looked straight at me, his eyes glaring into mine. He glanced over at Cooper next to me, and scowled.

"Looks like Peacock isn't too happy about me sitting next to you," Cooper joked.

"He shouldn't care," I said. "After all look at all the girls surrounding him," I gulped. "Not that I'm using you to make him jealous. That never even crossed my mind, and I'm no way into that kind of game. It's immature and childish, and I refuse to stoop to Drew's level."

Cooper laughed. "So that's what's going on between you two. I kinda sensed you knew him from the way you were talking about him and staring at his back."

"We, um, just broke up, more on my part, and…"

"Oh," Cooper said. "That explains that look he had on his face when he glared at me just now."

"I'm so sorry, Cooper," I apologized. "You must think I'm a real mess, but, I hate that you're already brought into our mixed up complicated relationship."

"No apologies needed, really," Cooper said. "I understand. I was in a relationship just like it not too long ago, and believe me, it can mess you up bad if you don't have friends to help you through it."

"You too, huh?" I asked, looking up into his earnest face. Who would break up with such a nice and gorgeous guy like Cooper.

Cooper took a deep breath and exhaled. "I'm still trying to get over it."

"How long ago?" I asked.

"A few months ago," he said. "Our relationship got so complicated, circumstances got in the way, and now…" he sighed, "I'm afraid I walked out on the best thing that could have happened to me."

"I'm sorry to hear that," I said reaching out to hold his hand. "If it makes it any better, I feel the same way."

"Thanks, Summer," he said wistfully.

My breath stopped, and my heart skipped a beat. For a moment, when he said "Summer", I thought I heard Nat's voice.

I shook my head. It couldn't be Nat, and he was nowhere near me. Maybe it was because I was wishing so badly last night to see him again at Drew's place. Maybe it was because I dreamt about kissing him and nearly making love with him last night. My dream seemed so real, I felt as though I did see, feel, and touched Nat.

"Hey, are you alright?" Cooper asked. "You kinda spaced out just now."

I shook my head again. "I'm fine. I thought for a moment, I heard the voice of a dear friend of mine."

"Oh," Cooper said, "Must be someone really special."

"He is!" I beamed. "No one can take his place in my heart."

Cooper smiled. "I bet he would be happy to hear you say that to him."

"I tried, but it's complicated."

"The story of my life, too," Cooper said.

"So, Cooper," I grinned, feeling like I've met someone who understood what I was going through. "I think you and I being here was meant to be. If you ever need to talk to someone, you can call me." I handed him my number.

"I will," Cooper said. "Thank you. And of course, you can do the same with me."

"Alright!" I giggled. It was loud enough to carry to the front row, and Drew's head turned around so quickly, I was afraid he would have whiplash.

"Oh, looks like Peacock heard you," Cooper nudged me. "If you do need to put him in his place, serve him his own medicine, I'll be happy to help."

"You don't have to, and that's not what I want to do," I said.

"I just don't like him flaunting all that in your face, especially since you said you just broke up. Any guy should have the decency to respect the relationship you once had by at least keeping all of that flirting to himself."

"Sounds like Drew has a thing or two to learn from you," I said.

Cooper narrowed his eyes at Drew, clenching down on his jaw. "Just because he's now wearing an expensive Armani suit doesn't make him a gentleman."

"So," Professor Knapp's voice carried over to Cooper and I, "That is the end of our session today. Be sure to read the first five chapters of your book by next class. We may have a guest speaker, and I would like for you to get the most out of his lecture."

The class dismissed, and I grabbed my bag, placing my tablet which I'd taken notes, in it.

Cooper stood up, and held out his hand to me. "May I?"

I smiled. Cooper was such a gentleman. I took his hand and he pulled me up to face him. Like I thought, he was tall and solid, like in solid muscles. He would definitely give Drew competition.

Speaking of Drew, as soon as I was up and smiling at Cooper, Drew had bounded up the stairs to stand next to Cooper, glaring at me and him.

Cooper gave me a look. "Do you need me to walk you to your next class?"

I glanced over at Drew, whose glare had turned into a look of despair. "Summer," he said, "I need to talk to you."

Cooper waited, crossing his arms like he had all the time in the world.

I was about to place my hand on Cooper's elbow to tell him, "let's go," when Drew grabbed my wrist.

"Drew…" I said looking down at his hand.

Cooper uncrossed his arms and stood up next to Drew, letting him know his presence.

Drew dropped his hand, and slumped down. "I only wanted to talk, Summer. Alone, just us two." He glared at Cooper.

I looked down, remembering everything that happened between Drew and I last night, including how he made love to me. I blushed. "Okay," I said.

I turned to Cooper and said, "Thank you."

"No need for thanks," Cooper said. "Call me if you need me." Then he took off.

Chapter 9

<u>Drew</u>

It still gets me bad when I see other men sniffing around Summer. I know she's beautiful inside and out, has the prettiest face I've ever seen, and a body like a Victoria Secret model so she will be attracting guys like bees to honey without even trying, but she's mine. She may not think so at the present, but she has and will always be mine.

"Summer," I said, after that too good-looking hunk standing next to her left. I had so much I wanted to tell her, but just seeing her angry at me, with her arms crossed, and instead of the warm adoring smile she always gave me, there was a scowl on her face, my mind went blank.

"Yes?" she asked.

My plan of getting her jealous, of forcing her to react to me, to acknowledged me, to even notice me in the class I saw we were taking together; back-fired on me. She was no longer buying my bad boy one-night-stand act that the other girls ate up. In fact, when I thought about it, she never did. She always saw through it. She always saw through me.

I was seriously at my wit's end.

I ran my hands over my face, looking down. "What can I do to get you back into my life, Summer?"

She uncrossed her arms, bringing her arms down. Her face was no longer filled with anger as something like compassion took its place. "Drew," she said softly. "I want to have you in my life. I truly do, but you keep doing something like this every time I get close to you."

"Summer," I said filled with remorse, "this was stupid. I'm sorry. I didn't mean to get all these girls throwing themselves at me like this in front of you. I…"

"You can't help that," Summer said.

"I know so I'm glad you understand that it's not my fault…"

"But you could help the way you reacted to them. You didn't have to flirt back. You didn't have to let that President Sorority chick tongue-kissed you in front of everyone," Summer said.

My face was hot with shame as she recalled everything that just happened an hour ago. I was so stupid. How could I have done all that when all I wanted was to get Summer back? Now she never wants anything to do with me.

"Drew…it makes doubt what we've had, what you said to me last night, that you love me…I don't know if you mean it or I'm a conquest for you, another warm body for you to fuck."

God, I really screwed up.

"You're not, Summer. None of those girls…no one else means more to me than you. You have to believe me."

"Why can't I believe you anymore, Drew?" she cried, the tears flowing down her cheeks freely.

My heart broke watching her cry, yet I wasn't sure if she wanted me to touch her. I wanted to wrap my arms around her, to kiss away her tears. I wanted to take away all the pain I've caused her.

"Summer, please don't cry."

"I can't help it," she whimpered. "I cared so much for you, but now…I can't even trust you. I feel as though I've lost another person I loved so much…Aunt Sookie, Nat, and you."

"Please Summer," I wrapped my arms around her, pulling her tight into my chest as I held her with my dear life. "I'm sorry. I'm so sorry for everything I've done to hurt you. I don't deserve you, I know, but I can't let you go. If I do, you might as well kill me. Without you, I am just a fragment of myself. You make me whole, Summer. You mean so much to me, you've got to believe me."

"Drew," Summer said, wiping away her tears. "I'm trying…"

"Please Summer, at least let's be friends. At least let me into your life as a friend. I won't push you into anything."

"I don't…"

"You let that guy sitting next to you be a friend," Drew said jealously. "You don't even know him, yet he's already friendly with you, laughing about everything during class. I could hear you from where I was sitting, and…Summer, if you think that guy just wants friendship from you, you'd better think again."

"Drew!" I scolded. "Cooper's not looking for a relationship right now. He's trying to get over his last one…the love of his life, so in a way, he's perfect for a friend," I said.

"Cooper?" Drew asked. "You call him by his first name now?"

"What name should I call him by? His last name?"

"No, it's just…"

"What?"

"Okay, I'm jealous. I'm jealous of any man or anyone getting close to you."

"You can't be, Drew," I said. "I have to have other people in my life…I no longer belong to you."

Her words sliced through me like a sword, and I felt myself almost stumbling back.

Summer was mine. How could she say she wasn't?

My entire body aches with an unquenchable desire when I'm near her. Just the sight of her, the smell of her, brings out all those alpha male tendencies. Like a caveman, I wanted to possess her, take her, parade her around as my woman.

My finger traced the skin on her neck up to her ear, and gently rubbed it. I felt her body shudder against mine. I love touching her behind her ear. I love that little shudder she does when I've found one of her erogenous zones.

Did she say she no longer belong to me? Maybe with her mind, but her body tells me otherwise. Yes, she still belongs to me.

She stopped crying and just let me hold her, rubbing her behind her ear, letting her lean into me. Her body temperature had risen, and I can see her face flush.

Oh, she was aroused. My male hunter's instinct tuned into that spicy but sweet scent I knew too well.

"I…" I began.

"Don't talk," Summer said, closing her eyes and shushing me.

I did what she commanded and continued touching and massaging her. Perhaps if this was all she wanted from our relationship for now, I could live with that. I could happily supply her with a constant source of Drew loving.

Maybe that's all she wanted from me…my body.

Again, I could live with that.

"Why can't I stop wanting your touch, Drew?" Summer asked.

"I could guess a million reasons why, Summer," I said, "but how about, it's because you and I have incredible chemistry. Try as much as we did to suppress it, it's there."

"Yes," Summer sighed. "It's there."

"About this friendship thing, Summer," I began. "It includes benefits, you know, well, on my part at least. You can do whatever you want with me. I'm fine with that."

"You are, are you?" she asked.

"If you want to jump my bones, I'm more than happy to oblige."

"I thought you'd say that…"

"So until we resolve this trust thing between us, until we figure out what I need to work on in order for you to take me seriously as the man for you, I propose having an arrangement where we satisfy each others' sexual urges and needs when we have them, with no strings attached. We're not married, not engage, and not dating; but we have needs, and we can't deny how much our bodies crave each others'. What do you think?"

Summer was silent, which made me worried. She was thinking this through, and when she thinks anything through and let common sense take over, it's usually a 'no'.

I increased my rubbing behind her ears, and bent down to lick the sensitive area.

"Remember how good it felt when you came last night? Remember how long I can hold you up and devour your sexy sweet pussy? How I love sucking on it?"

"Oh Drew," Summer moaned. "You're so persistent."

"Yes, I am, Summer," I breathed into her ear. "Especially when it comes to you."

I stuck my tongue into her ear then and traced her lobe. "Dammit, Drew," Summer muttered. "You drive a hard bargain. I can't tear myself away from you."

"Is that an 'yes'?" I asked.

"Yes," she moaned.

"Good," I said. "It's settled. We have an arrangement, and whenever you need me, I'll come running, and whenever I need you…"

"We'll see, Drew," Summer said. "Whenever you need me, find me."

Chapter 10

<u>Summer</u>

Drew and I parted after our so-called arrangement, and I went back to the Pad, eager to begin my work for the Sociology class.

I got through chapter three but was having a hard time understanding the theory behind chapter four and five. I wasn't sure if it was too early to call Cooper, to ask him if he'd started reading, but I really wanted to get all my reading done before I forgot.

It was the secret behind me getting straight A's and me maintaining my scholarship at USC. I was studious.

I punched in Cooper's number, and waited for him to answer.

The phone rang and rang, and I was about to hang up when he picked up. "Hello?" his velvety voice said. He sounded like he was in the middle of something.

"Hi Cooper, it's me, Summer!" I said brightly. "Sorry to disturb you, um, are you in the middle of something? I could call back."

"No, no, it's alright," Cooper said. "What's going on?"

"I'm embarrassed by this, but I started reading the chapters for our next Sociology class and I got to Chapter 4 and couldn't understand the theory. I mean, it's supposed to be easy, right? But I just don't..."

"Oh, don't worry about it," Cooper said. "I just finished reading the chapters, and it wasn't as easy as everyone thought it'd be. So, what do you not get about it?"

"The concentric circles," I said.

"Ah," Cooper said. "That was complicated. Got some time to go through it?"

"Yes," I said. "It's the one thing holding me up before I can finish my assignment for Sociology. You see, I'm a bit of a nerd…I need to get my homework done first thing after class so it's still fresh in my mind, and if I wait, I forget."

"Sounds like me, Summer," Cooper said wistfully.

I stopped. Again, Cooper reminded me of someone familiar just now. Nat? Aunt Sookie?

"Did you see how that diagram showed the impending eco-growth?" Cooper asked.

"I saw it, but I don't get it."

"I have to show it to you in person so you can see how it works," Cooper said. "Do you want to set a time to meet?"

"I'm at the beach all day today," I said.

"Must be hard," Cooper joked. "I'm actually heading out there to take some photos. Which beach are you at?"

"Malibu. I'm a few blocks from Errol King's Oyster House. Want to meet there?"

"Good, ate there a few times before. I know where it is," Cooper said. "I'll be there in half an hour."

"Okay," I said, hanging up. For some reason, I was smiling to myself after the call. Something about Cooper seemed so comforting and familiar, he gave me the kind of feeling I felt when Aunt Sookie was alive.

I changed into white shorts, a black tank top, and got ready to go to Errol King's Oyster House, which was across the street from the beach and a short distance away from the Pad, but I took my SUV, an inheritance from Aunt Sookie just in case I needed to take off from the restaurant.

Arriving at the restaurant, I walked in and found Cooper already seated at a booth, his text book from class laid out in front of him. He was dressed in a grey non-descript t-shirt and grey cargo shorts, with a dark zip-up hoodie covering his hair. "Hello Cooper," I said, sliding into the bench across from him. "Thank you for meeting me on such short notice."

"Hey Summer," Cooper said. "Nah, it's no problem. I was heading out to the beach anyways. I needed to get some footage in for my project."

The waitress came by and handed me a menu. I looked over at Cooper, and he took a sip from his soda drink. "I already ordered," he said.

"Oh, then I'll have the fried oysters and clam chowder," I told the waitress. "And a glass of water."

The waitress nodded, gathered my menu, and walked away.

"So Cooper," I said, "what kind of project are you working on at the beach?"

Cooper smiled a slow smile that was endearing and charming. "A documentary," he said.

"You're a filmmaker?" I asked.

"I want to be. I've always enjoyed acting, but I'd rather work behind the scenes."

"What a small world," I said. "I have an acting school I inherited from my aunt...Aunt Sookie's Acting Academy."

"No way," Cooper laughed. "I took some classes there when I was really young."

"You were probably there before Aunt Sookie got the Donovans and me into it."

"Probably," Cooper said. "I just remembered what an amazing woman your Aunt Sookie was. She got me into acting and now filmmaking because I had so much fun in her classes."

"Oh Cooper," I said, feeling happy to hear about Aunt Sookie's positive influence on a child who had since grown up into a fine young man. "You don't know how much that meant to me."

"It's all true," Cooper said.

"Even better," I joked.

"Yes, definitely better."

"So, what's the documentary about?"

"A bunch of things. It's hard to talk about it," Cooper said. "I feel like once I talk about it before it's finished, I would lose some of the story."

"I see," I said, not really seeing. He was a true artist, like Astor.

The waitress came by with his dish, a lobster ravioli dish, and mine, the fried oysters and clam chowder.

"Smells delicious," I said when she left. I pushed my dish towards him and said, "You can have some. I like sharing with people when I'm eating."

"I noticed," Cooper said, taking one of the fried oysters and biting into it. "It's good," he said.

"I know," I bit into one piece and felt the juices run down my mouth. I stuck out my tongue as far as it would go and slowly licked the juices from my chin and the corners of my mouth. When I was done licking my lips, I noticed Cooper had stopped eating.

He was staring at me with such a wistful expression…sad and soulful. There was something there, too, his aquamarine eyes were gazing intently on my swollen lips with hunger.

It made my stomach flutter with the intensity he was staring.

"Is there something wrong?" I asked.

Cooper shook his head. "No, nothing. I was just thinking about how much you remind me of my ex-girlfriend."

"Oh, I'm sorry," I said.

"It's okay," Cooper said. "That's one reason why I'm making this documentary. It's a way for me to find closure. For her sake and mine…we both need to move on."

I could see how heart-wrenching it was for Cooper to talk to me about her, and that made me want to reach out to him. "Hey, if you want to talk about it, I could listen."

"That's very sweet of you," Cooper said. "I don't really want to, but maybe you can help me through this by working on the documentary with me? It's actually for a film class project I'm doing, too."

"I'd love to," I said.

"Thank you, Summer," Cooper said. "This means the world to me."

"Anything to help," I said.

"Now eat up, Summer," Cooper said. "It takes a lot of energy to think through some of the concepts introduced in Chapter 4 of the text."

I took another piece of fried oyster, and felt the juices run down the sides of my mouth again. I must look like such a messy eater.

Before I could lick it off or wipe it away, Cooper's fingers beat me to it, wiping the juice from my mouth with his finger, then licking his finger clean.

Oh. My. God. That was so unexpected. Yet so sexy.

"I've acquired a sudden craving for oysters," Cooper said, his voice low and sensual. "You don't mind me having another piece?"

"Not at all," I said. "Have it all." I shoved the dish closer to him.

He picked up one piece, bit into it, swallowed, and stuck out his tongue to lick the opening of the oyster with long savoring strokes, while his eyes watched me.

The way he was looking at me made me think he was thinking of licking me that way.

"Oh, Cooper," I said, feeling my body grow warmer. "I…"

"Delicious," Cooper said, popping the entire oyster into his mouth and chewing.

"Yes," I said. There was some truth with oysters being an aphrodisiac because how would that explain that sudden white hot chemistry between Cooper and me.

"Do you need some fresh air?" Cooper asked.

"It is getting hotter in here," I said.

We quickly finished the rest of our meal and gathered our things. Without the waitress coming back with our check, we headed to the cashier. I pulled out my wallet, but Cooper placed a hand on me, indicating he would pay.

He pulled out his wallet, and opened it, revealing a thick bunch of cash bills.

Without much thought, he handed the cashier a hundred dollar bill and told her to keep the change.

Then he took my hand in his and walked me out of the restaurant. Once outside, he didn't let my hand go immediately, but kept holding it. "Sorry, I needed some fresh air," he said.

"I know."

"So now we walk to the beach from here, and we can talk about those chapters."

He took his backpack from his car, and held out his hand to me, which I took before leading us to an isolated area on the beach.

From his bag, he pulled out a blanket, laid it on the sandy beach, and sat down, bringing me down onto the blanket next to him.

"Now that we're nice and cozy," Cooper said, "Here's the Sociology book, and the diagram of the Eco-center Push." He explained the diagram in the most clear and easy-to-understand style until I understood it well enough for me to explain it to him.

When we were done going over the textbook, I asked him. "What were you planning on doing at the beach today before I called you?"

Cooper pulled out an expensive professional camera, jumped to his feet, and started taking pictures of everything at the beach. He even took a picture of me.

I lunged at him, trying to grab the camera, while he kept dodging me. Then he began running down the beach with me in hot pursuit.

He was fast, but I was faster. When I finally caught up to him, he was grinning widely. "I knew you were fast," he said. "But I'm fast, and if you are able to keep pace with me and even outrun me, you are pretty darn fast!"

"And quick like a stealth," I said, reaching behind him and around him to try to get his camera. I tickled him under the ribs to get him to drop the camera into my hands. Then using his own camera, I took snap after snap of him.

By the time we headed back to our cars, we were sweaty but happy.

"Bye, Summer," Cooper said, hugging me as he walked me to my car. "I'll see you soon."

"Bye," I almost kissed his cheek, but pull back. What was I thinking? I've just met the guy yet I felt as though I've known him for a long time.

Chapter 11

Summer

I met with Cooper again at the beach the following weekend after having lunch again at Errol King's Oyster House.

We worked on shooting footage at the beach, and I helped film a bit of him talking about the beach, talking about the history of Malibu and how there were pirate caves hidden all over Malibu.

"Summer," Cooper said. "You're a natural in front of the camera. How about I film you sharing what you love most about this place? I want to capture the essence of a place by showing how a place can affect people."

"Oh, Cooper, but this is about your story, your view. It shouldn't be about me. I'm not the star of your documentary."

Cooper put his hands on my shoulders and brought my chin up to look into his eyes. "Summer, since I met you, you've opened up an entirely new way of life for me. You've become a part of my world so what you say about this place, matters to me."

He leaned in close, and I closed my eyes. I've just met him, but our bond has been so strong, it felt as though I've known him all my life.

I waited for his kiss and waited. I opened my eyes to see Cooper staring at me, his eyes full of sadness.

Was he thinking of his ex-girlfriend?

Was he still heartbroken and unable to move on?

Since spending more time with Cooper and getting involved in his documentary; I was able to step away from Aunt Sookie's Academy, from Drew, and even Rachel for a while, and not get consumed with the turmoil I felt from all of that. I needed some time and space away from them, just to clear my head. Cooper had been the medicine I needed to help me heal from the loss of my family – Aunt Sookie and the Donovans.

But was I ready for another romantic relationship again?

Was I ready to start something with Cooper, although both of our hearts have been broken recently?

Cooper made that decision for both of us by dropping his hands from my face and stepping back. "Um, I'd like very much to have your commentary on this beach, this place, and what it means to you, Summer. I know it holds a special meaning for you so I want to capture that love and passion you have. It is that love which makes a place thrive. Without it, it is like a plant without the sun, and it will wither and die."

I smiled. "Sure, Cooper, I will be honored to be part of your film. But I'm not even dressed for it. I mean I'm just wearing a tank top and shorts. I don't even have makeup on."

"Trust me, Summer," he said, using his finger to tuck a strand of hair behind my ear, "You don't need anything else to make you beautiful."

My heart jumped for a second before settling down. Cooper just called me beautiful.

"Are you sure?" I asked. "I mean I know how the camera tends to wash people out and..."

"You are perfect the way you are, Summer," Cooper said.

My heart jumped again for a second time, as my mind had a moment of déjà vu thinking where did I hear something like that once.

My Perfect Summer.

It was what Nat called me in his last letter to me.

At that realization, I was brought back to the state of mind when I read it. Elation that Nat was alive, sadness for finding out he was alive just to have him walk away from me forever, and anger for not telling me earlier, for keeping secrets from me.

"Are you alright?" Cooper asked leaning in.

"I'm just remembering a few memories about my ex and…"

Cooper wrapped his arms around me. "Try not to think about it. It can overwhelm you if you delve on sad things. Besides, you're here to give me moral support, right? Quit thinking about yourself, and help me film this documentary," he joked.

"True," I said. "I…"

"No, 'I' this," Cooper scolded me. "It's 'Cooper, where do you want me to stand?' 'Cooper, how about if I say this?' 'Cooper, can I get you anything since you look parched, and ready to keel over from thirst?' 'Cooper…how about we stop by my place and I invite you in so we can get to see what makes Summer tick?' 'Cooper…'"

"Are you trying to tell me something?" I asked dryly.

"Focus on me, Summer, and you won't go back into that place of darkness. I don't want you to go there, and as someone who cares about you, I will be there to help you through it, just like you're doing this for me."

"Thank you, Coop," I said, leaning my head on his chest. "I needed that."

"Coop?" Cooper asked.

"Yeah, it's short for Cooper. I think it's time I start calling you by your nickname."

"Do I need to have one?" he asked.

"I tend to give nicknames to people I have an affection for," I said. "So, you're Coop."

"And you're Sum," Cooper said.

"Yup!" I laughed.

Cooper ruffled my hair with his hand and pulled me in close for a hug. "You're crazy, you know that?"

"So I've been told."

"Crazy, beautiful, funny, passionate..." Cooper's eyes roamed around my face before settling down on my lips.

I made a face, sticking my tongue out, hoping to be as silly as possible to break his gaze or I would be in serious trouble wanting him to kiss me.

Cooper laughed. "And adorable."

"I'm trying to live up to my namesake," I said. "Being all sunny and happiness…you know being Summer."

"You don't have to try," Cooper said softly, his fingers back up to cup my chin. "You are."

"Uh huh," I squeaked. Damn he was so gorgeous and sexy staring at me with those expressive beautiful soulful eyes.

He was staring at me again as though he was trying to decide what to do. His expression grew from soulful to darker in a matter of seconds.

Oh uh…now it was my turn to keep him from going down the rabbit hole.

"Hey listen Cooper, my house is just a short walk down the beach. Let's go there. I can freshen up for the filming, and you can get something to drink. I think you mentioned you were parched?"

That broke his gaze from my lips and he smiled slowly in a way that again made my inner lustful self say, "Hot damn that man is scorching hot."

"Alright, Summer," Coop said. "Take me to your palace."

I grabbed his hand, and pulled him through the sand towards the Pad. I think I knew him well enough to trust him knowing where I lived. We reached the steps leading up to the house, when he stopped, looked around and grinned happily.

"It hasn't changed," he muttered.

"What?" I asked.

"Oh, just talking to myself," he said.

"You look like you recognize this place," I said. "Have you been here before?"

We walked up the steps past the pool and into the house where I led him to the kitchen. "If you sit here, I'll get you something to drink. What do you want? Soda? Juice? Water?"

"I'll just have water," he said looking around.

I got a glass out of the cupboard, added some ice, and filled it with a bottle of water from the refrigerator. I turned around to hand Cooper the glass, but bumped into his chest. I almost dropped the glass, as Cooper steadied me, took the glass and placed it on the counter next to him.

"You scared me," I said a little shook up.

"Sorry I snuck up on you. I was just wanting to lend you a hand."

"It's alright," I said into his chest. God he smelled good. Masculine, clean, and a little musky.

He looked down at me, "Summer…" he began, his eyes filled with pain. "There's something I…"

I held my breath.

"Oh hi!" Rachel walked out of her room with a duffle bag. "I was just heading out. I booked a commercial, and it's up at San Fran so I'm flying there right now."

"Rachel!" I went to her. She didn't smile, and I didn't blame her. It had been awkward between us, when I broke up with Drew and refused to talk to him for weeks, which she was against.

"Um, Astor will be at the Academy covering for my class so…"

"That's nice of Astor," I said, actually relieved I did listen to him and sold a part of the Academy to him.

"Yeah," Rachel said carefully. "Astor's been incredible. It was a shame how you had to break up with him."

"He broke up with me," I said.

"Whatever. He's too nice of a guy to deserve having his heart broken."

"What?"

"Well, hopefully he'd be different once I come back from San Fran," Rachel said. "Because it seems, you've already moved on from him, from Drew, and even Nat!" She glanced over at Cooper who had taken a seat at the kitchen island…the seat Nat usually sat in when he was here. How appropriate, I thought.

For a moment Rachel seemed frozen as she looked at Cooper. Then she shook her head. "Nah, it couldn't be."

"What couldn't be?" I asked.

"Never mind. I must be just seeing things. Anyways, I'm outta here, and um, whoever you are…"

"Cooper," I said.

"Nice to meet you," she said. "Just know you're in line with some pretty amazing guys for her so if you even want a chance with her, you treat her right, not like my knucklehead brother Drew." With that, she walked out the door.

Despite whatever was going on between me and her, whatever was going on between she and Astor, or even with Drew; I still loved her like a sister. And she still had my back.

Cooper had an amused grin on his face as his eyebrows cocked up in a question. "So…what's going on with her?"

"She's my best friend from babyhood, and she lives with me here now that she's going to USC for her freshman year. But she and I...we just went through some pretty heavy stuff, not just about my ex, who happened to be her twin. And my other ex, who happened to be her older brother. I think me not being with either one of them had strained my relationship with her."

Cooper smiled. "Rachel, is it? She seems pretty tough yet vulnerable inside. I can understand what she's going through, but in the end, it's your life. You can't live your life to please Rachel. In the end, whomever you end up with will be your choice and no one else's. Give Rachel some time. Check up with her, talk to her, be her friend and sister. It seemed she needs you more than she let on."

I nodded. "You're so wise," I said. "Are you sure you're not an old man in some hot young guy's body? Oh, did I just say that?"

Cooper laughed. "So you think I'm hot?"

I blushed.

He came up to me and took my arms in his hand, leading me to sit on the sofa next to him. "Do you think I'm as hot as that Peacock in class?" he whispered close to my ears. "I have to admit, Sum, I find you pretty hot yourself…"

"I'm…"

The front door opened, and I jumped up from my seat. Who could that be?

A beautiful woman in her mid-40s with long flowing chestnut hair and green eyes walked in. She was clad in a khaki linen suit that flattered her trim athletic frame. From how glamorous she looked, you wouldn't believe she was an officer in the army, but in special intelligence.

"Mom!" I cried, running to her.

"Summer!" she said, hugging me tight. "I still can't get over how big you've gotten while I was out fulfilling my missions."

"Are you going to stay before taking off again?" I asked. "I mean…"

"I know what you mean," she said, patting my cheeks. "I have some time off, but I will be sent off again. It's my call of duty."

"I know. I understand," I said.

"I'm just glad you got a chance to grow up with your Aunt Sookie when she was alive," she said. "She was a remarkable woman, Summer. I see a lot of her in you, and I'm glad she rubbed off on you like you were her own child."

I gulped, not wanting to cry, remembering Aunt Sookie, her illness, and her sudden death.

"But duty calls in another way," Mom said. "The Donovans. We're very close, Summer, you have to remember that. They've helped me out so much when I needed help, like getting me back home to you this last time, so I'm going out there to help take care of Nadine. Since Nat left and since Drew moved here, she's now being taken care of by a live-in nurse. Nothing against that nurse, but she's not family so I'm going there to stay with her for the next few week or even a month or so before I get sent overseas on another mission."

"That'll be what Mrs. Donovan needs," I said. "Yes, you should go. Don't worry about me."

"I came here to see you and to tell you where I'm going. I also see you seem to be doing just fine. I know you are. We Jones women, we're from pretty strong stock, you know," Mom said. "Aunt Sookie, myself, and you. We are survivors, don't you forget that."

"I won't!" I hugged my mother tightly.

"Good, because, Summer there will be days when it's tough and you don't know how to go on, as well as the most happiest days in your life, so what you need to remember when faced with the ups and downs, is that it will all work out."

"Thank you, Mom!" I said. "I'll remember."

"Good," she said, wiping at the corner of her eyes. She noticed Cooper then and stood up straight. No one will get to see the soft side of Major Jones if she can help it.

"Hello," Cooper came up to shake Mom's hands. "So nice to meet you Mrs. Jones. I now know where Summer gets her beauty and strength of character. You must be so proud of her."

"I am," Mom said, looking Cooper up and down. She had a quizzical look on her face as she stood back to take Cooper in. "Have we met before?"

"No," Cooper said. "I tend to look like everyone's best friend, ex-boyfriends, or sons so that's probably why you think I look familiar."

"Okay," Mom said, still looking confused. "Well, I'm late for my flight, but I'll call you, Summer, and let you know how things are going in San Fran."

"Keep an eye on Rachel, too," I said. "She's going up there too for a while."

"Ah Rachel," Mom said. "I will. Nice to meet you Cooper, and please, don't let Summer get you down. If she does, do what makes her happy and she'll come around!"

My face was red then. "Thanks, Mom!" I shut the door, and faced Cooper.

"Nice family you've got there," he smiled. "You are indeed lucky."

Chapter 12

<u>Nat</u>

Ever since that night I visited Summer at the Pad, I've been sorely tempted to reveal myself to her, to take her back into my arms and ask her to forgive me, to be with me the way we were before I left.

When it comes to Summer, she can break down any barriers I've erected. Any resistance I have set up, comes crashing down when I hold her in my arms, when she looks at me with those eyes full of love.

Visiting her that night made it loud and clear for me that I can't leave Summer alone. She had taken sleeping pills…not to kill herself with, but because she needed them to sleep. Anxiety? Insomnia? That wasn't Summer. She never had to use anything to go to sleep. She was always on the go, full of energy, non-stop energy that she expended on volleyball for school, teaching and running Aunt Sookie's Academy, and studying for school. They kept her so busy that by the time she fell asleep, she was bone tired.

Someone like the Summer I used to know never used sleeping pills.

So it alarmed me. Summer wasn't taking care of herself. She wasn't sleeping right. She wasn't eating right. She wouldn't let Drew in to check on her, too, I bet. And Rachel? Drew was supposed to eventually let Rachel know about me, but I have no idea if he had.

When Rachel gets angry, she expresses herself through clothes, through her hair. She doesn't actually hurt herself by starving or not sleeping. Rachel, as much as everyone underestimates her, loved herself far enough to not let her body go. She wasn't self-sacrificing like Summer was. And she had Drew to fall on. As much as the twins dissed on each other, they were also their greatest supporters.

So, of course, I was worried about Summer. I could feel her loneliness even when all I did was sleep next to her that night. I was just going to talk to her, check up on her, and leave, as Drew requested. But I couldn't. She needed me then, and I couldn't leave no matter what.

So, I made the call.

A call that may change everything.

"Hello Lamar?" I said into my phone. I had swept my place earlier this evening, making sure there weren't any bugs or surveillance anywhere.

I've been doing this since I moved into my low-profile condo. Upon entering my condo, I sweep the entire place before I could let out my breath and relax. When I found a suspicious-looking device buried into my roommate's plant at the dorm, I knew I couldn't live in a dormitory with roommates and no privacy. Not with the kind of danger I was in.

So now in my small condo, looking out to the ocean, with a clear view of the beach, I can live in peace, yet still feel like I was part of the place I grew up in with Summer...the Pad. The place wasn't cheap, but it was a few blocks away from the Pad, and from where I was on the top floor, I could even see the Pad's beachfront backyard, see Summer's car in the driveway, and the front door.

In other words, I chose this place so I could still watch and protect Summer. Drew didn't even know it. Lamar didn't even know.

"Hey kid," Lamar said in his deep booming voice. He suited his position well...an FBI handler who had arranged and organized everything for me to disappear without a trace so I can start my life all over again without being Nat. "What is it?"

"When can I reveal myself to Summer?" I asked. "When can I have my old life back?"

"Ahh, so this is what you called me for," Lamar said. "I know it's hard for you with this new identity, but proceedings are going too slow. You have to hold on a while longer. But there is another matter, and you calling me now is good timing. This news literally just came up this afternoon."

"What is it?" I asked.

"Word is out that one of the top bosses, Xavier, has escaped and had entered the U.S. seeking revenge, especially for the guy who shut down his center overseas. And guess who that guy is? You. So, now's not a good time to come out and announce to the world, 'Hey World, Nat's back!' especially when these guys were able to get a photo of you. You don't even know how grave your situation is, do you, kid?"

"I have some idea," I said. "It's grave enough you guys had to kill me off so they won't come after me."

"You do get it, then," Lamar said. "I figure you would since you're a genius, but when it comes to matters of the heart, you're vulnerable, and that vulnerability can get you, your father, your mother, your brother and sister, and Summer killed."

My heart dropped hearing Lamar hit it on the head with what I was thinking. I was being led by my love for Summer to risk getting my entire family killed, not to mention anyone associated with me. There was no way I could reveal my identity to Summer and my family now.

"So, this Xavier…what does he look like?" I asked, ready to arm myself against him if I ever see him.

"That's the thing with these criminals. They are hard-core enough they change their looks with plastic surgery every once in a while. The last time anyone has spotted him or surveillance camera had picked up on him, he was dressed down, blending into whatever culture and country he was in. Mostly in non-descript shorts and t-shirts. I'll send you a virtual postcard with his face in a crowd. He's the third from the left edge. Third from the bottom edge. And we'll make it easy for you to get a license to carry weapons. You will need one just in case. These guys mean business so if you have to defend yourself against them, you will at least be equipped."

"That would help," I said dryly.

"Good we need you to stay alive, Nat. You are providing a great service to your country and internationally. Your genius and expertise is rare. We will take good care of you, no doubt. Are you fine with your new identity?"

"I wasn't at first, but things are getting better," I said.

"That's good you're blending in and adjusting," Lamar said. "It makes your cover believable."

"I am definitely blending in," I said, not mentioning how I was able to visit Summer at the Pad without her seeing me.

"Good, blend in, and before you know it, you will be a new person, safe to roam anywhere you want to go. Beats having you sent to a witness protection program or get accompanied by security men all the time"

"Alright Lamar," I said. "In case you didn't know, I moved out of the dorm and into my own condo for safety's sake."

"I know," Lamar said. "That was fine. Like I said, being in your situation you're free to roam and live life as you once did, but only as your new identity. Moving to a condo is your own choice, and at least you can have privacy again, instead of being at the dorm. Good thinking, Nat. Now if you'll excuse me, I have to go. Until next time!"

"Until next time," I said hanging up.

As soon as I ended the call, another call came through. "Hey Nat, there's been a break-in at the Academy."

Drew.

"Any idea who was behind it?" I asked.

"No, that's why I'm checking it out."

"Taking any men with you?" I asked, meaning some of our security men from Donovan Dynamics.

"Probably when we get the entire place wired for a new security system installation. You should be there to get your fingerprints scanned so you are cleared in the system."

"Don't worry," I said. "I'll find a way to handle that."

"Suit yourself," Drew said. "Anyways, I got some news about Summer…she's been hanging out with a guy who seem a bit mysterious. A classmate of hers. Don't know how far into this relationship she's been, but they are moving fast."

"Don't concern yourself with who she is dating or seeing, Drew. It'll drive you crazy. Just make sure she's fine, and if the guy isn't for her, she'll figure that out quick."

"You're taking this all pretty calmly." Drew said.

"There isn't any other way I can take it right now."

"Okay, well, I hope to see you soon, Bro."

"Me too," I said.

When the call ended, I breathed a sigh of relief. Drew didn't suspect a thing.

Chapter 13

Summer

Drew called me the following day after my weekend helping Cooper film.

"Summer," he said. "I want you to know, there's been a break-in at the Academy, and I think the security system we installed had been compromised. I'm heading there to check it out. I thought you should know."

"I'll go with you," I said. After all, Aunt Sookie's Academy was my responsibility. "Thank you for telling me."

"I know you're busy and all, and that you have other things on your mind, so I wanted to take care of this for you, Summer," Drew said. "But if you want to come out to the Academy, that's up to you."

"I'll go," I said. "I'll see you there in 15 minutes."
"Okay," Drew said. "See you there."

I quickly changed into jeans, a tank top and my leather jacket, grabbed my purse and keys, and headed out to my SUV. Thanks to it being late at night, there wasn't much traffic, and I was able to arrive at the Academy earlier.

I walked in and checked out the door. It didn't seem as if it had been tampered. Yet, thanks to Donovan Dynamics' sensitive security system, it triggered an alarm that notified Drew, who was in charge of the system. I turned on the lights of the old theater which was converted to an acting school, and walked around, trying to see if anything looked like it was out of place.

The front room which was the lobby seemed like it had always been for years. I walked into the classroom, which was the theater's main room consisting of the stage, seating, and an area behind it for concessions. Nothing seemed different.

Now I had to go into the back rooms where Aunt Sookie's office was, where it had become my office. I shouldn't be nervous about going in there, but last time I did, I found my computer hacked with warnings from a stalker named Sloane on the screen.

And also, the attack…the one where I was nearly raped by Sloane. Until Drew came in, fought Sloane off, and saved me.

Drew…Drew…Drew, how we went through so much together. How he had always been there for me.

I walked to the very spot where I was attacked and had been forced on my back to the ground, and Sloane was pressing down on me, breaking my arm…

A sound.

My skin suddenly got goosebumps.

My hair stood on ends.

I couldn't breathe. What if it was Sloane who had come back to finish me off?

It couldn't be, he was sent to jail, or so I thought. I never did see what happened to him. I didn't want anything to do with him after his second attack on me at the USC campus.

I trusted Nat and the authorities to put him away.

Drew was too distraught and shaken up to handle it. He nearly killed Sloane, and I was in no condition to face him, either.

Another footstep.

I bolted up from where I was kneeling on the ground checking out some strange residue and ran straight to the hallway only to run into something hard and solid. Then arms came around me, trapping me in place.

"No, let go of me!" I cried, struggling with all my strength. "You are not going to attack me again!" I cried and screamed, remembering the terror I felt when Sloane had cornered me, threw me to the ground, and started forcing himself on me.

"Summer! Summer, it's okay. It's me. Drew." Drew's soft but assuring masculine voice stopped my struggling, and I leaned into his chest, feeling instantly relieved but so tired.

"Drew," I said wearily, "You're here."

"I'm always here for you," Drew said, stroking my hair to calm me down.

"I thought…I thought you were Sloane," I said, shaking at the thought of seeing Sloane again.

"No, it's me," Drew said. "It's too bad you got here before me. I was going to check out everything to make sure it was safe before letting you come in here by yourself after the alarm system was tripped."

"I got here early, and I just thought I could handle it. I mean, I'm a big girl, right?"

"It's okay to let someone else handle it, Summer, if you don't want to…" Drew said. "You don't have to play the strong independent woman with me, although you are. Once in a while, you can let someone else handle things, could you?"

I nodded, hating to admit that I could.

"Sloane…" I said, "He did a number on my psyche. I never admitted it or try to show fear, but…Drew…I get panic attacks sometimes…especially when I'm alone, and…"

I started crying, hating myself for being so vulnerable, especially around Drew. What is with me and Drew? He brings out the part of me that I always try to hide.

"Summer, it's okay, Summer," Drew said, kissing my temples, kissing my eyelids. He wrapped his arms around me so tightly I could feel his heart thundering next to mine.

My shivering went down, and I nestled closer to Drew. "I don't know what I'd do without you, Drew."

"I won't let you find out," Drew looked into my eyes before crushing his lips on mine. I kissed him back hungrily, as his tongue lightly touched mine, sending an electric thrill through my entire body.

"Drew…"

"Don't talk, don't think, Summer," he said. "Just be with me right now." He deepened his kiss and I was lost in it, feeling his love pour into me.

We kissed and kissed, forgetting everything else around us until Drew's phone went off, and we pulled away from each other.

"Summer," he said, almost as out-of-breath as I was. "I have to get this. It's Donovan Dynamics."

"Okay," I said, walking back into the office area to continue checking if anything was missing or suspicious.

None of the files were missing or rifled through. The desk drawers were locked.

I turned on the computer and checked if anything had been opened or tampered with.

Drew came into the office and saw me open a tab that had been in the history. It was a search on Cooper Sorrento.

"What? Why would anyone be searching for Cooper here…" My first suspicion came from the one person I didn't want to suspect…the person standing in front of me. Drew.

I turned around to look at Drew. "Have you been here lately?"

"I was here this weekend," Drew said. "Rachel asked me to come in here to pull her acting resume and portfolio from the computer for her shoot in San Fran. She was in a hurry and couldn't come in herself."

"So you were the last one using this computer?" I asked.

"I guess, unless someone else did. Why?"

I showed him the search on Cooper on the computer, and looked at him.

Drew's face said it all. He looked surprised that I found his trail, but embarrassed. "Summer, I just wanted to see what kind of guy you were hanging out with. I know I sound jealous, but…"

"You do, Drew," I said.

"I checked him out because I was looking out for you," he said. "You don't know if he could be another Sloane, Summer. You don't know anything about him, yet you're spending so much time with him…"

"Drew, he's a friend and…"

"Summer, we were friends. Best friends. You confided in me about everything, even about your crush on Nat."

"That was before we grew up," I said.

"I miss that, Summer. I miss being your friend. I loved being your lover but it just seemed I can't satisfy you. I'm not enough for you even though I've tried to be. I've tried so hard to be the kind of man you want me to be. I've tried to be like Nat, I've tried to be just a casual lover, and even propose a just sex arrangement, but even all that…you have doubts about us. Maybe, Summer. Maybe…I finally realize now, I'm not the guy for you. Maybe it's time for me to accept that and stop pursuing you. I wanted to be with you so badly, but maybe it's not in the stars for me."

I was almost speechless, but as I watched Drew ball his hands into fists in determination, I knew he was dead serious.

"Speechless? Nothing to say?" Drew asked roughly. "I was right then. You never loved me for me. You will never give your heart completely to me. Well, I can't have that, Summer. I want to be with someone who loves me and only me. I'm sorry, truly sorry it worked out this way, but now I know, and...you're free to date anyone you want...Cooper even. And I'll move on, too."

With that, he left me abruptly, without giving me the chance to speak or catch up to him.

Ch. 14

<u>Summer</u>

Drew left in such a hurry, I couldn't catch up to him. He was clearly upset, and I was too.

"Wait Drew!" I called out, getting out from behind the desk, and almost tripping on some of the cords underneath.

"Darn this!" I tried to untangle the cords from my shoes, but one of them had gotten entangled in the mess of cords. By the time I got out from behind the desk, leaving one of my shoes and raced to the front of the theater to the lobby and to the door, Drew was gone.

"Drew!" I cried, feeling a hollowness at the pit of my stomach. I felt like a part of me was torn out. "I have to let him know it's not true. I love him, and not just because he was trying to be someone else for me. I love him because he's Drew."

The silence that greeted me when I talked to myself out loud made it clear I needed him no matter what. Even if whatever we have between us turned into friendship again or as lovers, I can't imagine a life without him.

Plus, dear Drew…I was worried about him. It had never been confirmed, but since Drew was Nadine's son, he may have inherited her mental illness. That was what Nat had been worried about before. Although Drew acted irrational or highly emotional at times, we still didn't believe he was like his mother…

I called Drew.

He wasn't picking up.

I texted him.

ME: Drew, I need to talk to you. Please don't feel this way. I do care for you.

He didn't answer me back.

I had to go find him then. I hobbled my way back to the office where I left one of my shoes underneath the desk, untangled it and got ready to go after him.

As soon as I walked out of the office and into the hallway heading to the theater's main room, all the lights went out, and I was in pitch darkness.

My first instinct was to scream but I didn't. The second worse fear I've ever had was being in pitch darkness. My imagination always ran wild when I encounter it, and always to the worst scenarios I could imagine.

"Oh great," I said talking to myself. "Must've pulled one of the cords that connected to the light switch. Brilliant, Summer," I scolded myself.

Wished I brought a flashlight, I thought again.

I attempted to make my way up to the lobby through memory, thinking I could fix the light problem tomorrow when it's daytime, but now I needed to get out of the Academy and go find Drew.

I made my way almost through the main theater area when I bumped into something hard and clearly didn't belong along the path. Not Drew again, I thought.

"Hello?" I said, up against the hard body in front of me. I felt so blind in the dark, not able to even make out an outline in front of me.

Silence.

"Okay," I said, "this isn't funny. Whoever you are, can you please move out of my way. I couldn't very well see you to move around you so you have to."

I heard an intake of breath and then a soft chuckle.

My hair stood on ends as I realized that didn't sound like Drew.

I was about to turn around to run the other way when hands came down on my arms. "Summer," the velvety soft voice said almost a hair-breath away from me.

Oh I knew that voice. So very well.

Nat.

My arms went around him, and I pull him to me to rest my cheeks on his chest. "I missed you so much," I cried.

His arms went around me to hold me tight. "I'm not supposed to be here," he said. "I'm not supposed to see you but I couldn't resist. Drew told me there was a break in here, and I wanted to check it out for myself, make sure things were safe, before you or Drew would get here. Looks like my timing had been off."

"I don't care," I said. "It's fine. You're here, and I'm safe with you. I'm here with you," I said, unable to believe I was holding, touching, and talking to Nat. "I never thought I'd see you again!" I couldn't hold back the tears now. "I thought you died."

"I know. I know," Nat said, kissing the top of my head. "I wanted to tell you so badly. I wanted to let you know the truth, but even now, it's too dangerous. You can't even see me."

"But you're here!" I said.

"By accident, and even then, I'm someone else."

"What do you mean?"

"I can't be Nat with you anymore, Summer."

"Why not?"

"We could be blood-related!" he said. "I could be Aunt Sookie's son...your cousin. What would people think?"

"I don't care what people think," I said. "I love you, and you love me. Couldn't we be together based on that?"

"Not as Nat, Summer."

"I used to think it matters, but didn't aristocrats and royalty marry their own cousins?"

"Does it matter to you?" Nat asked.

"No, it doesn't. I just want to be with you," I said, nestling my face closer to his chest. It hit me minutes ago, I was in the same position with Drew. Oh Drew!

"What about Drew?" Nat asked, as if he could read my mind. "How do you feel about him?"

I wanted to answer him truthfully but I couldn't. I didn't even know how I felt.

"Seems you're not sure yet," Nat said. "That's what I thought. No, actually, I thought by me being away, you and Drew could sort out your feelings, but I see it's still the same as when I had left."

"My feelings for you haven't changed, though," I said, reaching up my arms to circle behind his neck. "I've always loved you, Nat. I still do." I pulled his face down to mine, and kissed him.

At first he didn't kiss me back, which scared me. Didn't he love me anymore?

I kissed him harder, using my tongue to open his mouth to touch his. I deepened my kiss, using my tongue to trace his teeth before tangling with his. Then I pressed my body harder against his, rubbing up against his crotch with mine.

I was about to pull away when he hadn't responded but Nat stopped me with his hand. "Don't," he said. "I'm just relishing your kisses and your touch. It's been a while since I've felt you. I still can't believe it's you."

"Oh Nat!" I cried crushing my lips on his, pressing harder, and tearing open his shirt so that I could feel his warm smooth chest. "You smell good, and…" I licked his nipple, which caused him to groan. "Taste so good."

I licked him down until I was bending down, unbuttoning his jeans as fast as I could, and pulling it down, releasing his thick throbbing hard-on. "You can't hide your excitement to see me, can you?" I said before taking him in my mouth.

"Oh Summer!" Nat groaned. "God, I've almost forgotten how good this feels with you. I've tried putting away all these memories of you, but…God this is so hard to resist."

I continued licking and sucking on him while he started involuntarily thrusting. Finally, he pulled me up before he almost climaxed, kissed me hard on my lips, while he pulled my jeans down, bent me over, and entered me. We both groaned throatily as he thrust and I met him with each thrust.

"Summer," he said breathily. "I'm coming."

"I'm there, too!" I cried as we both climaxed at the same time. Our bodies kept the pace as we exploded, and I still wanted more of Nat afterwards.

He held me tight and kissed me afterwards on my lips and my forehead. "I didn't want to do this the first time I see you again, but…"

"I want to feel you, see that you're alive, Nat." I said. "Making love with you is the only way I could feel you deep inside of me. That you are a part of me. That you are alive, and throbbing with life inside of me."

"Summer," Nat kissed me. "I will always love you no matter how I express it. That," he chuckled, "was incredible."

He helped me stand up, and fix my jeans before he cleaned himself off and pulled on his. "Are you afraid of the dark now?" he asked.

I laughed. "Not if it was used like that."

"I agree," Nat said. "You would probably be confused if you saw me in the light."

"Why?"

"I don't look like the Nat you remembered. It's all part of my new identity."

"Okay, then," I said. "I can live in the dark if I can be with you. If it's the only way for me to be with you, I will overcome my fear of the dark."

"I hope it isn't the only way you can see me," Nat said. "I hope I can bring those guys who are out to get me and anyone I care about, to justice so I would never have to hide away from you again."

"I'll help you, Nat," I said. "I'll help you put them behind bars."

"Too dangerous."

"Don't worry about me. I'm already involved. I get the feeling so is my mother and even Aunt Sookie. I need to help you out or we will never be free."

"Then come with me," he said, leading me in the dark back into the office area as easily as if there was light. He went to a switch and pulled down and up. Before long, the light began fading in, and...Nat...Nat stood before me in the light and as someone else...

Cooper.

"Cooper?" I asked. "You're Nat?" I almost fainted. Then it hit me. All the clues. Cooper saying he took Aunt Sookie's acting classes when he was little. Cooper happily filming the beach and telling me how he loved the place. Cooper walking up to the Pad and looking at the Pad with love in his eyes. The way he made me feel when I was hugging him. The way he spoke to me, as though he was wise beyond his years. The way I would see him looking at me when he thought I wasn't looking.

How he would say things that reminded me of Nat.

"Oh Nat!" I cried, running up to him and into his arms. "I thought I was crazy feeling something for Cooper, but…now I know."

"Now you know, my Perfect Summer. "You are and will always be my Perfect Summer."

"And you will always be my Nat in Shining Armor." He bent down and kissed me so hard I knew my lips would be swollen.

Ch. 15

<u>Summer</u>

I thought that would be the ending to my Summer chronicles. That I would end up with Nat, but fate had another surprise in store for us…and like so many things in life, it doesn't always go as we hope.

We both heard a click near the doorway to the hallway we just came in from and turned.

"This is just beautiful," the figure holding the gun pointed at us said. Because of the lighting, I couldn't see who he was. "I get out of prison to seek my revenge on that Drew fellow who would've killed me if Summer didn't stop him, and find the missing Nat Donovan. Do you know there's a bounty on you, pretty boy? Not nice to cross the head of the cybercrime syndicate. Now it looks like I'm getting the bounty now."

He approached us, then stopped.

"I could have sworn I heard Nat Donovan's voice. Now where is he?"

He took a step closer to us and another step until he was a few yards from me. Oh. My. God. My heart dropped. Sloane. Why and how did he get here?

"Still such a temptress," he said. "Summer Jones...how I fantasize about putting my cock into you." He leaned in closer and said, "I go through all my collection of photos of you...especially the ones where you're sleeping in bed, naked, waiting for one of your loverboys to come fuck you. I get so hard just looking at those photos."

"You disgust me!" I said.

"So it's okay for Drew or Nat to enjoy your luscious body but it isn't for the rest of us non-billionaires. Not-so-pretty types? You think you're too good for guys like me, don't you. Just like your Aunt Sookie."

"Quit tarnishing her name!" I shouted.

"Tarnish? She's tarnished herself. She's a whore, just like you."

"Not true at all," I said.

"Then what were you doing just now having sex with yet another loverboy?"

He looked at Nat.

"It's not like it looks," I said. "Plus a woman can be just as sexual as a man, it doesn't make them whores."

"But it does with you. Women should be pure, chaste, and clean until their marriage night. Otherwise, they are whores," Sloane said. "And if they get pregnant out of wedlock like your Aunt Sookie, they are a bigger whore."

Nat threw a punch at him then and knocked Sloane to the ground. "The one being the filthy dirty scum is you," he said in a deeper voice, the one he used as Cooper, punching Sloane again in the face. "You have no right to judge Summer, Aunt Sookie, and any women for anything. What makes you perfect?" Punch. "What makes you God? Only someone who is perfect can judge anyone else. And from the looks of it, you are far from perfect."

Nat threw another punch but Sloane caught his wrist and head-butted Nat who fell back.

"I don't know who you are, but you better mind your own business," Sloane said. "I have unfinished business with Summer and her two loverboys. One of them tried to kill me – Drew wasn't it? And the other one, Nat…got me time in prison. Luckily, thanks to some corrupt politicians, my guys got me out for helping law enforcement hack into child molester sites and sending them to prison."

"Trading one sick bastard for another I see," Nat said.

"So I'm free to go as I please and now I'm free to seek revenge out on Drew and Nat. Do you know there's a bounty on Nat Donovan? Pretty huge too. Not nice to cross the head of the cybercrime syndicate. Now it looks like I'm getting the bounty."

He approached Nat, producing a knife from his pocket. Nat kicks at him, but Sloane twists and grabs hold of Nat's leg, pulling him forward and down, causing Nat to fall.

"No!" I shout, rushing towards Sloane. He turned around and stabbed me in the side, and I fell to the ground. "Na…" I almost shout, but realized Sloane didn't know Cooper was Nat, and saw Sloane handcuff Nat to a chair, then turned to me to cup my face. "Since you've been doing the wild thing with him, you would know where Nat is, wouldn't you, Babe? But first, looking at your hot body, I'm not through fantasizing about you. That stunt you pulled with your three loverboys that got me into prison, only made me angrier and more determined to have you. Now, the first place I'm going to fuck you in is your office. Then..." he place his knife against my neck. "You will strip for me starting right about..."

Boooooooooom!

It sounded like a firecracker had gone off in the room, and I reached up to cup my ears.

Sloane had been kneeling over me, but now he was down on the ground next to me. A bullet hole in his head.

I looked over to the doorway heading to the hallway and saw Drew standing there, a gun in his hand, looking shock.

"He had a knife to Summer's neck," he said. "He was going to kill her."

I got up, clutching the side where Sloane had stabbed me. "Drew!" I said, trying to get to him. "It was self-defense. He had a knife to my throat, and he was going to rape me. He stabbed me, and…"

"About time someone got that Motherfucker," came a deep booming voice behind Drew.

A tall and muscular man in his late 30s stood behind Drew.

"Who are you?" I asked, wanting to protect Drew. If this was the police…

"I'm Lamar," the man said. "And no, I'm not with law enforcement. I'm with the FBI." He looked over at Nat handcuffed to the chair.

"Lamar," Nat said. "I had to see Summer…and if I haven't been here to check out the Academy, Sloane would have gotten to her earlier."

Lamar gave Nat a pointed look but said, "I'll talk to you later, but now, what do we do with these two?"

My eyes grew wide, realizing that Lamar may not want me and Drew to have witnessed what happened to Sloane.

"It was self-defense," I said. "Drew was just helping me and Nat…"

"Nat?" Drew's eyes traveled to Cooper. "You mean…he's Nat?"

I closed my eyes. Now we were in trouble. I blew Nat's cover, right in front of the FBI.

"So you really didn't know?" I asked Drew.

"No, I was even suspicious of Cooper, how fast he moved in on you and how quickly you two were already friends…"

"Drew," Nat said, "I couldn't reveal myself to you, too. As much as I wanted to, I could only see you two as Cooper."

"The cover, it was so good," I said. "Nat acted like a Cooper, and he looked different."

"I used what I knew about stage makeup from what Aunt Sookie taught me at the Academy," Nat said, "And

Lamar changed my identity through forms, paperwork, etc. I was acting, Summer. Playing a role, bleached my hair for it, got more buff to fill out, wore contacts, and wore clothes I'd normally wouldn't wear. Something Aunt Sookie taught me again. Lamar helped me through it all."

"Nat's a rare guy," Lamar said. "Smart, talented, and very mature beyond his years. His situation is rare. We don't have cases like his where a civilian is brought in to take down a crime syndicate, and lived to live a normal life."

"Is that what Nat did?" I asked. "I thought he went to Afghanistan to help bring his father back. I didn't know he was there to do FBI type of work."

"Donovan Dynamics do government jobs, Summer," Nat said. "This one happens to involve my dad and also your mother."

"My mother?"

"She was handling investigation of an international cybercrime ring and was taken hostage, so my dad went over to try to get her out, but he was taken too. That's when I went…"

"So it was a matter of extreme danger and secrecy," I said. "I wished I knew. I was so worried. I would have understood and kept your secret."

"It's not my secret to keep," Nat said. "It was strict orders from the FBI. Still is…this thing here, was all a mistake, an accident."

"Sloane was connected to that cybercrime unit your mother was investigating," Lamar said. "The fact he got out because he helped some corrupt officials is horrendous. Look what might have happened. He went out to seek revenge immediately after he got out, and tried to rape and kill you."

"What can we do about this?" I asked. "If the officials who let him out were corrupt, then they would want to get his killer."

"I'll handle this," Lamar said. "That's what I do. I make people disappear. Alive or dead. But now you two know Nat's cover as Cooper. That puts you two in greater danger than before."

Drew and I looked at each other nervously. What was going to happen to us?

"As far as all my intelligence tells me," Lamar said. "No one knows Sloane was here. No one besides you two have seen Nat as Cooper. His cover is still safe…as long as you two can act like he is Cooper."

"I can do that," I said.

"Same here," Drew said.

"Will someone get these cuffs off me?" Nat asked. "I'm beginning to lose circulation."

"In a sec," Lamar said. "This is important stuff, Nat. Your cover could have been compromised."

"Not if no one knows Cooper is Nat," I said.

"If you let that out, remember, you two become targets of this crime ring who's after Nat," Lamar said. "And it's getting ugly. Sloane showing up here looking for Nat is a very bad thing. It means they got whiff that Nat is alive. That was one cover we created for Nat. Now the only thing keeping a bunch of assassins going after a bounty on Nat, is this cover. Sloane is just the beginning, I'm afraid. And he was an idiot. Other assassins wouldn't hesitate to shoot all of you, and ask questions later."

I gulped. Nat really was in big trouble...just because he was trying to save my mother. I owe Nat everything. I walked over to Nat, attempting to take off the handcuff. "I'm so sorry, Nat," I said. "I didn't know everything you were handling, including this. I didn't know how much you've sacrificed for me and for my mother."

Nat was silent as he looked at me with the most loving eyes. "It's no sacrifice, Summer. You were there for me when my world came crashing down. You've already lost Aunt Sookie and was so distraught, I couldn't let you lose your mother, too."

I cupped his cheek with my hand and leaned in to kiss him. "I love you, Nat," I said. "No matter what happens, I'll always love you, please remember that. You don't need to prove to me your love. You don't have to go risking your life for me."

"Guess you fell in love with a guy who still believes in chivalry, who still believes in being a knight to his lady. I will follow you to the ends of Earth for you, Summer. You should know that about me already."

"Even pushing me towards Drew," I said. "I love him, too," I said. "But it should be my choice who I want to be with, not because you gave up on me. I understand why, but I couldn't go through with it, although I loved Drew already."

Nat turned his head to the side to look up at a spot above me.

Drew and Lamar had approached us.

"Guys," Lamar said. "Time to get moving. You know the guys Sloane got word Nat was still alive? They're out in droves, searching for Nat's whereabouts. It's not safe here, at the Academy. It's not safe at Summer's house. Is there anyone staying there at the moment?"

I shook my head. "No, Rachel and my mother left yesterday for San Francisco."

"We'll make it so they stay there right now."

"Mom is there for a while anyways, but Rachel…"

"Rachel is into Astor Fairway?" Lamar asked.

"How do you know?" I asked.

"Most girls are…" Lamar smiled wryly. "Even my 7 year-old."

I couldn't help but smile.

"Astor is about to get called to San Francisco for a sudden promo blitz for his upcoming film," Lamar said.

"You could do that?" Drew asked.

"Like I said," Lamar said, "I make things happen." Lamar grabbed hold of the handcuff holding Nat to the chair and with one swift kick from his boots, broke it off. "Come on, guys," he said. Clean up whatever needs cleaning to show you weren't just here. Leave no trace."

He produced some rags from his bag, sprayed it with some cleaning agent and handed it to Drew. "Wipe the ground clean from where Sloane fell. And everywhere there is some blood, then put it in this trash bag."

"Summer, go clean up your computer. Better yet," Lamar went to the computer, unplugged it, and handed it to

Nat. "Carry this. We'll take whatever that can have personal imprint on there with us. Who knows what these guys will go through. How fast can Donovan Dynamics get here to install your newest baddest high-tech security system?"

"They're coming tonight," Drew said. "I'll text them to come faster."

"Right away," Lamar said. Lamar produced a plastic sheet from his bag, and wrapped Sloane's body in it. He hoisted him up and carried him to the lobby where there were standees of popular actors. He carried two of the standees and went out.

Drew followed him with the trash bag full of soiled rags. I fixed the chair Nat was handcuffed to and everything that seemed out of place. Nat joined me as I made my way through the theater's main room, lobby, and out. Lamar had packed a non-descript black van with the standees, Sloane's body, and the trash bag. He closed the van, and went to Nat, Drew, and I.

"This is where I say 'good-bye' until next time," he said. "You are all not to return to the Academy for a while. Nor Summer's house."

"What about the students and classes here?" I asked.

"The theater is closed for renovation. An email will be sent out tonight. They will come back when it's done."

"So where do I go if I can't go back to my place?" I asked.

"The Fortress," Lamar said. "The safest place in the U.S...Drew's place. Built like Fort Knox."

"Really?"

Drew looked embarrassed. "It's our data warehouse. That's why you don't see anyone there. And that's why I'm at the top floor."

"And Nat?" I asked. "Where is he going?"

"With you," Lamar said. "He'll keep you safe until you get to Drew's. And besides, he's Cooper, your new best friend."

I turned to Nat and smiled, relieved he wasn't going to be whisked away from me again.

"Come on," Drew said. "We better get going. Donovan Dynamics is coming now. I don't want them seeing Nat, um, Cooper here."

Drew got in his car and drove off, while I got into my SUV, where Nat loaded my computer into, and Nat hopped in.

We drove off, close behind Drew and away from Aunt Sookie's Academy and away from the Pad, heading to the Fortress.

"Summer," Nat said, "Sorry to drag you into this…"

"Don't say that, Nat," I said. "I want to be a part of your life no matter what. I'm just so grateful to have you back…you don't know how much I cried for you and grieved for you when I thought you'd died."

"Summer," Nat said. "I'm so sorry you went through all that. I didn't know how much it would affect you."

"You don't?" I asked. "You are my life, Nat."

"I thought you wanted Drew, Summer," Nat said.

"I was confused. I wanted both of you, love both of you, but even when I had Drew, I kept wanting you. Even when Drew changed to be with me, I realized he had changed to be more like you for me. It's you who I want, Nat. Always and forever."

Nat leaned over and kissed me on the cheeks. His cheeks were wet from tears. "This makes everything so much harder, Summer," he said. "I've put away so much of how I feel for you so I could be away from you. I don't know what the future will hold, but I know that you being with me will be dangerous. My life's in danger, Summer, and I don't want you to be put into danger."

"I can change and hide my identity, too," I said.

"No!" Nat said. "No, please," he said more gently. "I don't want you to change at all. What's the point when we have to hide who we are to be with each other? It's bad enough that I have to change, but I never ever want you to change who you are, Summer. Keep on being Summer for me, Summer. It's the memories of Summer that keeps me going."

Ch. 16

<u>Summer</u>

We made it to Drew's place without a problem. As soon as we entered the lobby and went up the elevator to Drew's suite, we were able to finally relax.

"That was intense," Drew said, grabbing bottles of water and handing it to Nat and me, before gulping one down. He was trying to stay calm, I could tell, especially at his own place, especially in front of Nat. But his hands were shaking, and I could see how his jaws were tensed. Poor Drew. I didn't know how I could possibly take back what happened tonight. Everything happened so quickly.

We both had planned on checking the Academy out, just a routine check, just two college students, just worried about classes, relationship issues, family obligations, and our sports or extracurricular activities.

Now things would never be the same again. Drew would never be the same again.

Although it was in self-defense, where it was either kill or be killed by the rapist/stalker, Drew had killed a person – a criminal, and he was shaken up about it.

"Nat," he said, "You can take my spare bedroom, and use my clothes. Last time I checked, we were the same size, but from the looks of it, you've been working out like your life depended on it."

"Well, bro," Nat said. "It kinda did. I was in training with the Elite group to be able to handle the physical part of the mission alone," Nat said. "I thought I was in good shape because of football and sports at home, but out there, you really have to be able to take it all – the elements, starvation, carrying heavy equipment all day, and being shot at."

"Man, I didn't know it was that brutal out there," Drew said, his eyes going wide and face in concern. "I bet you saw some real tough shit."

Nat nodded. "I did. Didn't think I'd make it out alive even, but I did, thank God!"

"I'm sorry," Drew said to Nat. "Man, I didn't realize how much you went through, and here I was enjoying life back home while you were being a man, a real man for Dad, Donovan Dynamics, the FBI, and Summer."

Nat got up and went over to Drew. "Don't be hard on yourself, Drew. Don't feel guilty. I chose to go. For me, it was the thing to do."

"I could've gone in your place if I had the training, and they got me up to speed. Then you could've stay back home with Mom, Rachel, and Summer," Drew said.

"If it was that easy," Nat said. "I had to go because I had the ability to break into their system and hack through their barriers to retrieve important well-guarded information. The Special Forces were there to help get me in and out as best as they could without getting me killed."

"So the FBI was involved?" Drew asked.

"Not until the end. That's where Sloane was involved, too. I got the FBI involved to put Sloane and others like him away. He wasn't just an ordinary perv, stalker. He was a hacker who was part of a crime ring overseas so I needed the FBI to help, plus I helped them get the names and identities of the cybercriminals."

"That's why this ring leader's after you?" I asked.

"That, and that I destroyed one of his branches, and took valuable intel from his system that sent him and his men to prison."

"What's his name?" I asked. "What does he look like?"

"Xavier," Nat said, "Here's a photo Lamar sent me of him." He showed me a photo of a handsome man in his thirties with dark hair and dark eyes. He was good-looking, but he looked dangerous and devoid of any kindness.

Drew came over to look at the photo.

"Wished they included height," he said. "You can change everything else about him through surgery, makeup, contacts, whatever, but you can't change height. I'm sure this guy has multiple disguises so he wouldn't look like that for long."

"Right," Nat said. "You can bet on it."

"So, in other words, we can't tell who to trust," Drew said.

"He can be someone from class, someone visiting the Academy, a mailman, pizza delivery guy…" I said.

"I was suspicious of Cooper at first," Drew said, looking at Nat. "The way you got close to Summer so quickly…"

Nat grinned. "Must be my charm, but it was because I already know Summer so well, I understood what she was going through and responded to it. Something, you still have to learn about our Summer, little Bro," Nat said.

Drew blushed, looking down.

I also looked down. As much as Drew had sexual experience with women, he didn't get them as Nat did. All it took was for him to pay attention to me, know what was bothering me, and sit back to hear, really hear what I was saying. But he was ruled by lust, as I was whenever we were together.

I looked at Drew. His hands were still shaking, and I knew that if he didn't get whatever was worrying him off his chest, he would have a hard time ever confronting it in the future. But he would have to be the one to want to talk. It was obviously something he had been harboring.

"Nat," I said, going to him. "Have you checked out Drew's security system here? I mean you're the mastermind behind Donovan Dynamics. Did you know about this building and how it was set up? Why is this such a safe place?"

Nat smiled an almost bashful smile. "It was one of my ideas to Dad. I said we needed a location away from our headquarters that was hidden and non-descript…a place just to store all the valuable information we're in charge of keeping, and to do it in a way that it would be secure from explosions, fire, earthquake, and spies. This place…" Nat looked around and stood up to walk to the glass window to look out onto the sleeping city, "was one of my dream buildings. We had the penthouse built on top for the family, if we needed it, and a couple of spare rooms. There is a kitchen commissary large enough to store a year's worth of food and cook for a hundred people, there are rooms of data storage units, guarded by the highest tech security we can dream of...so, to answer your question, Summer, I did know about this building even before Drew did. But it was never part of my plans to move here or to even stay here...only for dire emergencies....which I think this qualifies for."

"Then Drew staying here...is it prohibited or...?" I began wondering how Nat felt about Drew occupying this building, his building that he dreamt of and built.

"I'm fine with it," Nat said. "After all, I walked away from being a Donovan, remember. Someone's got to step into the shoes of leadership, and frankly..." he leaned in to whisper to me. "I'm ready to let someone else handle the demands of running Donovan Dynamics. I'm ready to go out and live my life, not as my father wanted me to, not because he put me in such circumstances that I had to be the man my mother relied on, but to really live my life as I've always wanted to…" Nat sighed. "In a way, me becoming Cooper Sorrento is a blessing in disguise. I'm discovering things I've never found time for and having a sense of purpose elsewhere besides Donovan Dynamics."

"So you're not sad about leaving your old life behind as Nat Donovan?" I asked.

"I was. I was devastated at first. How could I not be? It was all I've known. That life…was so well-planned for me, it was the easy and unexpected path to take. But was I happy? Look, Summer, you know me. You know what I went through. I was tortured, I felt guilty about everything, I felt responsible for everyone. I didn't want to live in San Francisco. I wasn't happy there. I wanted to be at the place I felt the most happiness, and that was here in Malibu with Aunt Sookie and you. I want that carefree attitude she instilled in us. She taught us to live life to the fullest, that although her life was cut short, she was happy. She lived a full life."

Nat touched my face and said, "That's what I wish for, for you, Rachel, and Drew. I know you've been pressured to make a decision between Drew and I…that your heart is torn both ways. I want you to choose me, but at the same time, I know we have time. You have a generous heart and you can't help loving us both and even Astor, but I see how distressed you are about deciding who you want to be with, and that if you choose one, you will be throwing away and ending a wonderful relationship with another. It's the hardest decision for you, Summer, and I think that eventually, you will come to a very clear decision without doubt. I'm sorry to put you in this situation. I'm sorry to even tried to decide for you by stepping away and letting you choose Drew, but the truth is, if you can't decide right now, if you are still torn both ways; please don't make a decision yet until you are sure. That's what Aunt Sookie would have wanted for you. That's what I want for you."

I was on the verge of crying. Nat had hit the nail on the head with how I was feeling. He knew me so well, and always knew what to say. I loved him so much, but I also knew that he could not go back to being Nat Donovan again. The innocence that was there for all of us had sailed. We weren't the carefree kids we were when Aunt Sookie was alive. That summer we all got back together at Aunt Sookie's Pad for the last summer before her death was the summer that changed everything. Nothing could be the same as it was before. Except in our memories, memories that we all shared together of those days playing pirate and princess on the beach, jogging and racing each other across the sand, and falling in love with every breath.

Nat again knew how I felt. He patted me on my shoulder, and said, "Summer, you know where I stand. I'll be fine with whatever happens. I'll also be there if you need me. We all will be…Drew, Rachel, and I. We all love you, no matter what." With that, he kissed me softly on my lips, and walked outside of Drew's penthouse. "I'll be checking out the security systems here in case you need me," he said hastily. I saw his expression, and it was calm, collected, and resigned, as though he had already prepared himself for whatever choice I would make considering him or Drew.

It made my heart pound faster as a million emotions and thoughts went through my head. How could I choose when I've loved both brothers since childhood? How could I choose and break the heart of the other? I wanted to be there for both of them. I wanted to provide the love they both craved and wanted from me. Despite what I said to Drew, I loved him as himself, whether it was the one-night-stand player Drew or the Drew who is now head of Donovan Dynamics. And Nat...he will always be the chivalrous knight for me, and for everyone else. He was so noble, he'd set aside his own happiness to fulfill his duties for others.

Drew had left to go to his room to change into his jogging shorts and t-shirt, his usual clothes, while I was talking to Nat. He came out with a bundle of clothes in his hand. "Here, Summer, since you didn't get a chance to get your clothes from the Pad earlier, you can change into my t-shirt and shorts to sleep in tonight. Tomorrow, we can go shopping or something," he said.

"Thanks, Drew," I said smiling. He was being so sweet, yet I knew something was eating him up inside. He handed me the clothes, and our fingers brushed, sending bolts of electricity straight through me.

Drew was equally affected as he let out a small gulp. "Is there anything else you need?" He looked almost embarrassed standing there…with a growing erection clear in his shorts.

Drew! Leave it to Drew to get aroused in the most inappropriate times, but here I was feeling my nipples harden looking at him. "Ah, where will I be sleeping tonight?" I asked. "I can sleep out here on the sofa…"

"No, not there, Summer," Drew said. "You can sleep in my room. I'd feel better if you do and not out here. What kind of a guy lets a girl sleep out here when he has a perfectly awesome bed for her to sleep in?"

I laughed. "Awesome?"

"Uh…yes, awesome, Summer," he said. "It's high-tech with rollers, massagers, warmers, and even music and sound."

"This I've got to see!"

"Oh, okay," Drew said, taking my hand and leading me to his bedroom.

I didn't see his bedroom last time I was here, instead getting hot and heavy with Drew out in the living room and by the front door. It was a good thing because it would have made me run.

"Drew!" I said looking around me. The room was covered in luxurious cream satin with chocolate-colored wood paneling on the wall. Expensive art adorned the walls, and a large blacken oak antique wardrobe stood in the corner. In the center of the room was a bed built on a circular platform covered with furs, satin sheets, and chocolate velvet pillows.

It was extremely sexy, luxurious, masculine, yet also feminine. I was impressed. But…the stripper pole in the corner as well as the black leather bench meant only for sexual positions and for fucking…was another thing.

"The other night you said I'm the only girl you've brought here?" I asked.

"You're the only one I cared to bring here, Summer," Drew said.

He took my hand and brought me to the bed to sit me down, and he kneeled down in front of me. "You're the only girl for me, Summer. All this is for you. All this is what I want to do to you. It's not even about sex, though, Summer," he said. "I would do anything for you. I would always be there for you."

I placed my hand against his cheeks, but he took it into both of his hands. "I love you Summer, and when Sloane held that knife to your throat, and I saw that you were bleeding, and he was saying all those filthy things about you, I had to stop him. I saw red, Summer. I shot him to stop him, and…" he started crying, "I'd do it all over again to keep you alive."

"Drew, oh Drew," I pulled him into my arms and hugged him tightly. "It's okay…"

"My body," Drew said. "I can't stop shaking."

"It was self-defense. If you didn't stop him, he would've killed me."

"I know," Drew said. "I know, but the reason why I'm shaking is not from the guilt. That bastard deserved what he got for terrorizing you for so long, for stalking you, taking all those private photos of you, for violating your privacy, for threatening you, starting all those rumors of you, to almost raping and killing you….I mean he had a long string of offenses. But the reason I can't stop shaking is the rage I felt against him and anyone who can think they can terrorize, cyberbully, and slander someone as sweet and loving as you, Summer. It's not okay that he got out of prison early. It's not okay he hardly serve any time for nearly killing you last time. It's certainly not okay that whoever let him out early think his freedom is more important than your life. He was let out of prison early just so he could go back to carry out what he didn't finish.

What kind of justice is that? And…I shudder to think what would have happen if I came a second later, if I hadn't turned back to go to the Academy to find you, to tell you I was sorry about what I had said earlier. You and Nat…would be dead!"

Drew ran his hand through his hair. "I know we've had our ups and downs. I know you loved both Nat and me so I don't want to make it any more difficult than it is. I love you like a man loves a woman. I crave you all the time, want you all the time, and I am always thinking about you. I decorated this room thinking of you, thinking how much I'd love to wake up every morning to see you by my side." He took a deep breath. "I also want to rock your world. Sex with me will never get old because this passion I have for you, is a constant eternal flame. While I may be the head of Donovan Dynamics, I would never do what my father had done to my mother, cheated on her with a mistress, and neglected us kids, sending us off to Malibu every summer or anywhere else but home. My top priority is you, Summer. You will always come first for me. Not my duties, not my work, nothing else. I just want to be back in your life, Summer. To have you smile at me with that adoring love in your pretty eyes. You are and will always be the most beautiful Summer to me."

He kissed me softly on my lips, while I kissed him back.

"I don't want you to make a decision about who you want to be with forever...me or Nat, but I do want you to know that I love Nat, too. He's my brother, and no matter what, no matter who you choose, we both will make an effort to live with it. Nat and I talked briefly, and we've agreed that the one you didn't choose will accept your decision like a man, and will not get in the way of the happy couple. So you see, Summer, we don't want you to feel tortured over choosing someone. We both want you to just be happy and safe. That's all we asked for."

I fell back on Drew's bed and looked up to the mirror above the bed. Boy, Drew's bedroom was equipped for non-stop sex and pleasure. There was no doubt he thought that was part of a loving relationship between a grown man and woman. That there was nothing ashamed about wanting to fulfill each other's needs in that area of a relationship. Although Nat had been upset when Nadine lost her mind and tried to kill herself over her impending divorce, Drew took to heart what could've made his father stray…what also broke down their marriage.

"It was sexual, you know," Drew said, as if answering my question. "Why my parents' marriage failed, and my father took on a mistress. They stopped enjoying and having sex with each other. As simple as that, it was that. I never want that to happen to us," Drew said. "We have those needs. It's there no matter what anyone or society says about it. As long as you and I admit we have this desire between us, and as a couple, work to satisfy each others' needs, along with emotional needs or whatever else you need from me, I never see our love for each other dying. Not like my parents' relationship."

"What about everything that went on between Nat and me?"

Drew took my hand in his. "Nat and I already discussed that our history and past could not be erased, and we never want you to…it's what makes you our Summer. While we may get a little jealous thinking about it, we can't dwell on it. What's more important is what happens in the present and the future. We love the same girl. With you, how could we not? We have to accept that many people will…you're Summer. You have that spark in you that draws people to you. We agree."

I nodded. Strange how the brothers…two men I love individually would discuss this with each other. I felt a little left out, but then again, that was how close Drew and Nat was.

I sighed again, scrunching my forehead in frustration. I never wanted to fall in love with more than one man, but I ended up falling for two wonderful ones. I never meant to have this love come between both men. And I certainly didn't want to separate Drew and Nat. They needed each other as much as I needed them. I took to heart what each had said to me, and thought with all my heart and soul what and whom I really wanted.

And I came to a decision….

Chapter 17

Summer's Letter to Nat and Drew

Dear Nat and Drew,

It was the hardest decision of my life, making a choice about the rest of my life, and with whom I would spend it with…

Two wonderful men who would give me the world, two amazing men who I would give the world to. It was rare even finding one love like ours, but two? Such a blessing.

I would've come to you separately to tell you my decision, but being with either of you always and still makes my head and heart spin…I love you both so much!

Aunt Sookie, on her deathbed, told me to be happy, and to live life fully. It is her advice that I will follow, and it is her will that I fulfill my destiny.

If I choose one brother, I will break the heart of another. If I choose one, I will not only lose a lover but a friend. Both of you have been family to me. Separating me from either one of you will be heartbreaking no matter what my choice is. I don't want to separate you two. You are brothers, and I know you will and should always be there for each other.

Yet I know if I walked away from either of you, you will be heartbroken as well.

There is no easy solution and no clear solution. Either choice, someone will get hurt. Either choice, someone will be unhappy.

The question is, what is the best solution? How certain are we of our love for each other? Can it stand the test of time? Are we in love with each other because we're in love with the idea of love or do we love each other for all our flaws and perfections? Are we good for each other? Do we build each other up? Do we complement each other and make each other grow? Do we satisfy each other? Do we challenge each other? Do we get along and have common interests, dreams or goals?

You see…so many factors to consider in deciding on your ideal love. Yet, the most important one to consider is...are we happy together, not does he makes me happy because happiness can be out of our control at times, but when we're together, when we're apart, are we happier people because of each other?

I hope I am all these things to you, as again, both of you are all these things to me.

Again if it is up to me, I could never make a decision. You are both my dear Donovan brothers, my family when I didn't have one growing up.

So this is my best solution for a solution. I want both of you. I love both of you. Call me selfish, call me indecisive, call me a two-timer, but as it is…I am living life to the fullest being with both of you. I am still too young at 18 to settle down and get married. You two are still too young to settle down and get married. You must fulfill Aunt Sookie's will too, to live your lives to the fullest.

Because of Nat's identity and dangerous situation, we've agreed we can't be together as we once were. Nat as Cooper is a dear friend, and I hope to stay friends to see how Nat will develop and live finally carefree of the weight he's always felt. Nat will always be a hero for me and for the greater good. I had always looked up to you, idolized you because you were so precious to me. Yet I feel your destiny is far greater than it will be with me. I want you to fly up to reach your full potential, to soar. It would be my greatest happiness to see you reach that potential and fulfill your true destiny.

And Drew…you've always been there for me uncannily at the right time. If it wasn't for you, I wouldn't be alive today. You are flawed, you have weaknesses like everyone else, and you drive me crazy all the time in both good and bad ways. We both idolize and care about Nat; we both fumble around together trying to be more like Nat. In more ways than one, I've come to realize you and I have more in common than we believed. I am insatiable like you are. I let my emotions run all the time, and I find sleeping in a bed with motors, lights, music and sound effects awesome. As Aunt Sookie has taught us, life is short, and I don't want to worry about the what ifs of tomorrow. I want to be with you right now. Today. And that's where we are until tomorrow.

Love your Lasting Summer

Epilogue

Nat

When I read Summer's letter to me, I found myself smiling. She had hit the nail on the head with what our relationship truly was. I was the big brother, the idol she never had, yet wanted to be like. Even writing a letter like the ones I always wrote her.

I should have felt sad or angry about her choosing to be with Drew but I also knew she was right about living life to the fullest. She was living hers, and so was Drew, but was I?

I missed certain aspects of my life as Nat Donovan, but I was beginning to enjoy the new one as Cooper or Troy or Bob or whatever cover I will have to have in order to keep ahead of Xavier and his cronies. It was an adrenaline-pumping adventure I never thought I'd come to enjoy…especially the part where I get the satisfaction of helping Lamar shut down an operation and put these guys behind bars.

"Will I ever have my life back again?" I asked Lamar. "Will I ever get to return to being Nat Donovan?"

"That's a sound iffy, Nat. For now, to keep yourself safe, and to be able to work for us to get this crime ring completely busted, you would have to be this other person. This is the way for you to still help Summer out, and still be close enough to her."

"But not as myself," I said. "When could I be myself with her?"

"When we bust this cybercrime ring, and bring all of them to justice so you, Summer, and Summer's mother are safe."

So as fate would have it, this was the way it would go, and Summer was smart enough to realize it. "Summer," I said to myself. "Thank you for letting me go fulfill my destiny."

Preview to Free Fall

10 Years Later

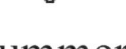

Summer

A Second Ending

I was 18 when I made the decision to be with Drew at the time, leaving Nat to fulfill his destiny with his new life and new identity. Little did I know at age 28, Nat and I would find ourselves together as we were when we were during that last summer I knew him as Nat. Drew assumed the helm at Donovan Dynamics and has been an even better CEO than his own father, much to everyone's surprise.

With that glory and victory came some steep danger and enemies. Now Drew is missing, and I need Nat to help me find him. Problem is, I don't know if Drew's illness had kicked in or was it truly something else. I don't know, but I do know that only Nat can help me find him, and despite the years we've been separated, I could still feel my heart race when I talk to him, I still feel like that little girl who worshipped the very ground Nat walked on when I think of him. We are not of an age to truly think about settling down – Drew, Nat, and I...now I will need to know everything between us.

Summer, Drew, Nat, Rachel, and Astor's story continues in

Book 6 of the Loving Summer Series

Free Fall (Loving Summer #6: Donovan Brothers Series #3)

*****

Find out what happens to Nat as Cooper Sorrento in a New Series Title to be Announced in *Free Fall*

Need to Talk to Other Fans about Loving Summer, Drewisms, Nat and more; join the Official Loving Summer Facebook Page at:

https://www.facebook.com/LovingSummerFilm

Yes! Loving Summer is going to be a Film!

OTHER BOOKS FROM KAILIN GOW

VISIT KAILIN'S WEBSITE to learn about new releases, the most awesome contests and parties, what Kailin and friends are doing in the community, workshops and events Kailin will be at and more at:

http://www.kailingow.com

and

on Twitter at: @kailingow